GUNS ALONG THE BRAZOS

GUNS ALONG THE BRAZOS

Day Keene

CHIVERS

British Library Cataloguing in Publication Data available

This Large Print edition published by BBC Audiobooks Ltd, Bath, 2008.
Published by arrangement with Golden West Literary Agency.

U.K. Hardcover ISBN 978 1 408 41229 9
U.K. Softcover   ISBN 978 1 408 41230 5

Printed and bound in Great Britain by
CPI Antony Rowe, Chippenham, Wiltshire

CHAPTER ONE

Plumes of dust trailed the hoofs of his plodding horse as Major John Royal, M.D., late of the Texas Sixth Army, rode into San Rosario after his three-day absence.

The waning Mexican sun was hot, the humidity oppressive. Royal was tired. He was thirsty. The patient he'd ridden out to treat had died. It wasn't the act of a gentleman to present a bill to a widow. Therefore, for the moment, he was almost without funds. Not that that made much difference. He had unlimited credit in every cantina in town.

After all, he was *el médico,* the only doctor within a radius of two hundred miles.

He tied his horse to the rail in front of the Golden Rooster and slapped the dust from his hat before entering. The dim interior of the cantina was gay with music and bright with female laughter. A company of soldiers were drinking at the bar and sprawled at the tables. Judging from the insignia on their dusty uniforms, Royal decided they were *Federales,* possibly a new garrison for the prison overlooking the sea.

He liked soldiers. He'd been one for five years. He set his battered medical bag on a table and with his six-foot-twoinch tall, two-hundred-pound bulk towering over them, he

1

joined one of the groups at the bar.

'*Buenas tardes, señors.* Welcome to San Rosario.'

Hostile silence greeted him. Don Jesus, the fat proprietor of the Golden Rooster, set a bottle of aguardiente and a glass in front of Royal. '*Norteamericano médico,*' he explained to the troopers. Proud of his English, he added, 'Major John Royal. Of the Confederate Army.'

The soldiers did not acknowledge the introduction. They were unimpressed.

Royal couldn't blame them. During the past few years, former soldiers of the Confederacy had become as common as fleas in the various Mexican states, and about as important to the country's economy. He knew two former colonels turned vaqueros, a captain tending bar in Sonora and a pink-cheeked lieutenant from Memphis who was selling lottery tickets on the streets of Mexico City.

Don Jesus spread his plump palms on the bar as Royal filled his glass. 'There was a man asking for you.'

'Who?'

The cantina owner shrugged. 'He didn't confide his name to me. But he talked and looked like a *yanqui procurador.*'

Royal drank his drink and poured another. He didn't know any Yankee lawyer. He doubted that the man was on official business. Not even the victorious blue-bellies would

2

have the colossal gall to attempt to extradite an obscure Texas major just because he'd refused to take the oath of allegiance. If the man had any business with him, it was probably connected with Cora or the ranch.

The subject was distasteful to him. He would always regret that he hadn't killed Cora and her Yankee colonel when he'd had the chance. Now he would never have another opportunity. It would always be a blot on his honor. There was only one bright spot in that picture—there were no children.

Royal dismissed Cora from his mind and applied himself to the bottle of brandy. He still wished he knew why his most recent patient had died. He'd done everything he could to save Don Sebastien's life, but for all its alleged progress, in 1869 modern medicine and surgery were still only a bottle of quinine and a scalpel's edge beyond the buffalo-dung poultices and incantations of a Shawnee medicine man.

The brandy failed to bolster his spirits. The thick adobe walls of the cantina gave an illusion of coolness that didn't exist. The soldiers smelled of stale sweat and horses. The shrill chattering of the cantina girls trying to sell their youthful favors to the soldiers sounded like so many greedy parrots fighting over scraps of rotten fruit. He'd come a long way in three years, all of it downhill. It was all so different from what he'd planned.

Royal debated taking the bottle with him and riding to his own small adobe at the foot of the path leading to the prison. At least it would be cooler there. He could lie in the hammock stretched between two tall palm trees and when night came he could look up at the stars and pretend he was still in Texas. He might even catch a few hours' sleep before a pounding on his door announced that someone had shot or stabbed someone else, that one of the prison guards had a bellyache or one of the cantina girls was in labor. It seemed that having babies was one of their occupational hazards. There were times when he was certain that during his three years in San Rosario he'd brought more bastards into the world than had marched with Sherman to the sea.

He compromised by carrying his medical kit and the bottle of brandy to an unoccupied table in front of one of the windows. It was a little quieter here if not any cooler.

The night grew darker. Don Jesus brought Royal a second bottle of brandy and lighted the candles behind the bar and in the brackets on the walls. The noise continued. The soldiers, reeling drunk now, quarreled with each other, joined in the fandango that started up and patronized the rooms in the rear of the cantina that had been set aside for that form of pleasure. From time to time one of the girls stopped in front of Royal's table, smiled her

4

unspoken question and went away disappointed when he shook his head. He couldn't remember a time when he'd felt less amorous.

He was halfway through his second bottle when he heard the voice. It was small and female and sounded breathless. 'You are *el médico?*'

Royal studied the girl with alcoholic interest. She was young, not more than seventeen or eighteen. Her face was small and oval and pale. The black mantilla covering her blond hair looked like it was of expensive silk. He'd never seen her before.

'That's right,' he admitted. 'Who are you?'

The girl's sense of urgency increased. 'I am Catana.'

'Catana who?'

'Catana de Sandoval y Olmedo.'

The name meant nothing to Royal but the company was nice. He indicated a chair at the table. 'Sit down. I'll have the Don bring us another glass and we'll get drunk together. Then—who knows?'

The girl remained standing. 'I am afraid you do not understand, *señor.* I am not of this place.' She glanced at the bag on the table. 'But you are *el médico?*'

'I said I was.'

'Then please to come with me—quickly. It is *madre mía.* She is in great need of medical attention and I have a carriage waiting

5

outside.'

Royal rose to his feet. He should have known by looking at the girl. She'd come to him because he was a doctor and he'd insulted her. 'I'm sorry. After you, *señorita.*'

'*Gracias, señor.*'

The girl smiled and started for the door with Royal close behind her, but before they could reach it a mustachioed officer jumped up from one of the tables and clamped his arm around her waist, attempting to swing her into the fandango in the middle of the room. The girl resisted and he pulled her closer to him and kissed her while the other officers at the table laughed uproariously at the girl's frantic struggles to free herself.

Royal set his bag on the table, tapped the man on the shoulder, and spoke rapidly in Spanish. 'I'm afraid there has been some slight mistake. The young lady doesn't work here.'

The reaction was not what he'd expected. The *mariachis* stopped playing. The chatter of voices ceased. In the silence that followed, the officer released the girl and turned, slowly, to face Royal. He sounded more puzzled than angry.

'You are speaking to me, *señor?*'

'*Sí.*'

'You are certain you have not made the mistake?'

Royal stood his ground. 'No.'

'She is your girl, perhaps?'

6

'No.'

'But you make it your business to speak sharply. You attempt to give me a lesson in manners?'

Royal wished he hadn't drunk so much. He didn't like the sudden turn in the course of events. He had no particular quarrel with this man but his pride demanded that he continue to stand his ground. 'You seem to need a lesson in manners.'

The other man smiled thinly. *'Gracias, señor.* I was afraid I was going to be bored in San Rosario.'

Still smiling, he fingered his mustache with his left hand while his right hand slapped the butt of his gun.

Royal's reaction was instinctive. He drew his own gun and fired before the other man's gun cleared its holster.

A puzzled look replaced the thin smile on the officer's face. His gun, still cocked, dropped on the hard-packed earth floor and the resulting jar sent the bullet under the hammer ricocheting around the adobe walls.

The puzzled look faded as a red splotch spread across the chest of his tunic. Then, lifting his empty hand as if to reach out and touch Royal, the Mexican officer coughed once and followed his extended hand to the floor.

The air in the cantina seemed suddenly withdrawn. It was difficult for Royal to breathe. He holstered his gun and knelt beside the fallen man and felt for a pulse. There was none.

Still kneeling, he looked up at the circle of faces glaring down at him. The blond girl who had sparked the incident was gone. In the distance he could hear the diminishing thud of hoofs and a creaking of dry carriage wheels.

'*Muerto?*' Don Jesus asked.

'Yes,' Royal said. 'He is dead.'

The fat cantina owner made the sign of his faith. 'This *would* happen in my cantina. Do you know who is this man you have killed?'

'No,' Royal said.

Don Jesus told him. '*Colonel* Valasques de Leon. The new *comandante* of the prison. He was to have taken over tomorrow.'

Two of the troopers helped Royal to his feet. One of the officers who'd been sitting at the table slipped Royal's gun from its holster.

'With your permission, *señor.*'

Royal stared back at the man without expression. He'd made a number of bad mistakes in his life. But killing a Mexican colonel in a country where the military ranked second only to God would probably be the last mistake he'd ever make.

CHAPTER TWO

By standing on his bunk and gripping the iron bars in the narrow slot that served as a window for his cell, Royal could see the red tile roofs of the town below and, beyond the town, the curved white beach and the ocean.

It made a pretty picture, almost as inspiring as the Brazos in full flood or his own fertile acres between the Nueces and the Rio Grande. Acres that he'd probably never see again.

After a flourish of bugles and a roll of drums, as required by Mexican law, *Capitán* Dijon, one-time French Foreign Legionnaire and current keeper of the prison, had read him his death warrant that morning.

Tomorrow morning they would march him out and stand him against a wall and shoot him. And that would be the last of the Royals.

Royal wondered, as he'd wondered a hundred times in the past three months, what had happened to the blond girl. His lips tugged into a bitter smile. Seeing him kill a man for her honor, *Señorita* Catana de Sandoval y Olmedo could at least have attended his trial.

He transferred his attention from the beach to the steep path winding up the cliff from San Rosario. It was nearing the weekly hour for visitors and the path was crowded with

9

laughing girls and women bringing baskets of food and drink and themselves to their men.

Royal mulled over the custom. The Mexicans were a practical people. Once a week, by law, the wife or sweetheart of each prisoner was permitted to spend an hour alone with him in his cell. In the event that a prisoner had no wife or sweetheart, for a few centavos, any of the cantina girls was happy to act as a substitute.

Royal released the bars and sat on his bunk. He had no wife or sweetheart or even a few centavos. However, he had not been treated badly during the months since his trial. Remembering the past favors they'd received from him, most of the prison guards had done what little they could for him. Only the female population of San Rosario had forgotten.

Now the women were passing through the big outer gate. Now they were in the courtyard being counted. Royal sat with his back to the stone wall, enjoying the sound of their voices. It would feel good to talk to a girl, to prove his manhood once more before he faced the firing squad. But it seemed he came out second best where girls and colonels were concerned. In the months since his trial and the review of his case, the only faces he had seen had been those of his guards and the women in the courtyard.

A key grated in the lock and the heavy door of his cell opened. He looked up, puzzled, then rose slowly to his feet. The guard standing behind the girl in the opening was happy for him.

'This week there is company for you, *señorá.*'

Royal studied the girl. She'd changed since he'd last seen her. Somehow she'd managed to make herself look incredibly wanton. Her lips were smeared with red. There was a smudge of dirt on one cheek. Her blond hair had been dyed black and hung down her back, Indian fashion, in thick twin braids. Her cheap white cotton blouse, cut low, and her equally cheap black skirt did little to disguise the perfection of her small, shapely body and the fact that they were the only garments she was wearing.

While he stood, wary and suspicious, she crossed the stone floor of the cell carrying a small wicker basket on one bare arm and lifted her face to be kissed as she clung to him.

'*Querido mío.* My beloved.'

She wasn't his beloved. He had small reason to even like her. If it hadn't been for her, he wouldn't be going to die in the morning. Royal started to push her away but she stood on her toes and pressed herself against him and whispered:

'Take me in your arms and kiss me. Pretend you are glad to see me. I *have* to talk to you.'

While the guard looked on with approval, Royal put his arms around her and kissed her. Her lips were firm and sweet. They tasted

11

wonderful. He ran one hand down her straining back. All of her felt wonderful.

The girl waited until the guard had closed and locked the door before she pulled away. Then her tense body went limp. Her eyes were more frightened than they'd been in the Golden Rooster. She slipped out of Royal's arms and took a step backward. Her voice was urgent.

'You will please to understand, *Señor* Royal. This is just something that must be done, whatever the cost to me. I am not a cantina girl. But I must speak to you on a matter of great importance and this is the only way I could get in to see you without arousing suspicion.'

Royal was amused. 'I'm sorry, Catana. But when a man has a date with a firing squad, only two things are important—a reprieve or a pardon. And don't tell me you have a pardon from *Presidente* Juarez in that basket.'

Catana shook her head. 'No.'

Royal sat back on his bunk. 'All right. Go ahead. Talk.'

The girl sat beside him, with the basket between them. 'First, perhaps, you would like something to eat.'

Royal had never been less hungry. 'No, thank you.'

She reached into the basket. 'Then a drink and a *cigarro*.'

'That I'd like.'

12

Royal drank from the neck of the bottle, then put one of the big black cigars between his teeth and lighted it with a wax taper the girl handed him. The tequila made him feel lightheaded. The harsh smoke tasted strange.

'You might have come to my trial.'

The girl folded her hands in her lap. 'Would it have made any difference?'

Royal was honest about it. 'No. I was dead as soon as I shot the colonel.'

'Because he insulted me.'

'That's the way it happened.' Royal drank from the bottle again. 'Now what is it you have to tell me? What is important enough to bring you here?'

'You,' she asked, 'are Major John Royal, late of the Texas Sixth Army of the Confederate States of America?'

'I am.'

'And you own a huge *rancho* in South Texas, near a small town named Dry Prairie?'

Royal smiled without humor. 'I did for a time. Ninety-nine square miles. My father got it on a Mexican grant when land in that section of Texas was still selling for thirty dollars a square league.' He added, 'Not that it's worth much more now.'

The girl gestured impatiently, brushing his cynicism aside. 'And when you returned from the war three years ago, there was an affair of the heart concerning a very beautiful but unfaithful *señora* whose given name is Cora? A

13

señora who thinks you are dead?'

Royal moved the basket from the bunk to the floor. 'How do you know so much about me?'

'I don't,' she admitted. 'I know nothing about you except you are a *Norteamericano* and a *médico* and you killed a man because of me. But there are certain questions I have been instructed to ask.'

'By whom?'

'Another *Norteamericano* who calls himself Jim Tyler.'

Royal had a vague memory of Don Jesus saying that some *yanqui procurador* had inquired about him. He asked, 'Is this man a lawyer?'

Catana shook her head. 'I do not know his profession. All I know is that he does not want you to die.' She lowered her eyes. 'Neither do I. That is why I am here.'

The tequila roaring in his head, after three months of enforced abstinence, Royal lowered his eyes to the rounds of soft flesh visible under the girl's sleazy blouse. He'd never wanted anything as badly as he now wanted this girl. She was one of the most exquisitely fashioned creatures he'd ever seen. But the more she talked the less sense she made.

No one cared what happened to him. Certainly no Yankee lawyer. Besides, no one, not even Jeb Stuart's Cavalry in its prime or the whole Texas Sixth Army, could pry him out

14

of a Mexican federal prison. All the time he had left was now. He drank from the bottle again and set it on the floor. 'All right. Let's stop beating around the bush. I don't know what your game is. I don't care. All I know is I'm to be shot in the morning.' He pulled the girl closer to him and slipped his hand into the neck of her blouse. Her heart was pounding as fiercely as his. 'All right,' he repeated hoarsely, 'what is it you have to tell me? What brought you here at this late date?'

He continued his explorations. The girl opened her mouth as if to protest, then thought better of what she'd been about to say as booted feet sounded in the corridor and the tier guard amused himself by peering through the peephole in the door of the adjoining cell and calling an obscene pleasantry about the amorous activities of the couple occupying it.

'The guard will look in here?' she asked Royal.

'Undoubtedly,' he answered her. 'You're the first company I've had.'

The girl continued, quietly, 'And if we're not . . . making love, he may be suspicious and report it to his superiors?'

'I'd say that was likely.'

Catana's eyes narrowed. Then she stood up and unbuttoned her blouse and slipped her skirt over her hips and dropped both garments on the floor of the cell. She stood nude, as if for Royal's inspection.

Her voice was barely audible. 'You like me?'

'Very much.'

She ran her palms over her body. Then, managing a certain dignity about it, she returned to the bunk and lay looking up at Royal. Her voice was very small. 'Then please to make love to me. But I do not wish to be raped. Please to pretend that I am your beloved.'

Still cynical, Royal asked, 'You know what you are saying?'

Catana continued to meet his eyes. 'I know.'

During the years since the war had ended, Royal had known a number of women, most of them cantina girls, but never one like Catana. After the first awkward contact and adjustment, it was like nothing he'd ever experienced. The girl was a fever, a fire. Whatever had motivated her to give herself to him, she wanted and needed him as badly as he wanted and needed her.

He never knew if the guard looked through the peephole or not. If he did, he wasn't disappointed. It went on for almost the full hour, with only brief intervals to catch their breath. Then, even after they were spent, he was still reluctant to lose physical contact. At the same time he'd never been more ashamed of himself. Looking into the big, black eyes inches from his, he said, 'I'm sorry, Catana. But if you didn't want this to happen, you

16

shouldn't have come here. After a man has spent three years trying to drink and wench himself to death, it's difficult to remember he was once a gentleman.'

She touched his cheek with the tips of her fingers. 'I made you happy? I pleased you?'

'You know that.'

She continued to finger his cheek. 'Then I'm glad.' She seemed to be choosing her words. 'Now please to listen to me and believe me. It may be that you will not be shot in the morning. Much money has changed hands and certain arrangements have been made.'

'With whom?' Royal asked her.

'With *Capitán* Dijon, the *temporero comandante* of the prison.'

Royal considered the information. It was well known in San Rosario that the renegade French captain would do anything if the price was right. It had been a matter of missing funds that had brought about his dismissal from the Legion. He asked, 'What sort of an arrangement?'

'Tomorrow morning at dawn you will be taken from this cell and placed against the outer wall of the prison. *Capitán* Dijon will be in charge of the firing squad. He will give the order for the execution. The men of the firing squad will shoot. When they do you will fall to the ground. But you will be unharmed.'

'The soldiers will be shooting blanks?'

'This I do not know. The details were not

17

entrusted to me. But you are to lie very still.'

'And then?'

'Dijon will pretend to give the *coup de grâce.* Then, when he marches the men back through the main gate of the prison, while the morning mist is still on the ground, you will make your way to the clump of trees at the far end of the parade ground where horses and an armed escort will be waiting.'

Royal was skeptical. 'I'm not saying it couldn't be done. But let's face it. No one in the States, either north or south, and certainly no one in this country, wants me alive badly enough to spend the money that would have to be spent to pay for a thing like this.'

Catana stopped his lips with a kiss. 'Trust me. Believe me.'

Long after the bugle ending the social hour had sounded and the line of wives and sweethearts was winding down the path to San Rosario, Royal still didn't know what to make of what had happened. Only Catana had been real. Clinging to the bars in the slot in the wall, he watched the girl's slim back and supple hips until she disappeared into the cluster of wild orange and ceiba trees halfway down the trail.

He'd never known anything more beautiful than the hour they'd spent together. He'd never felt so emotionally and physically replete. But the girl had to be lying. It had to be one last practical joke on the part of the fellow officers or the relatives of the Mexican

18

colonel whom he'd killed.

Releasing the bars, Royal sat on his bunk and tried to light *a cigarro* and failed. Reaction had set in and his hands were shaking so badly he couldn't bring the tobacco and the wax taper together.

CHAPTER THREE

The fog rolling in from the sea lay heavy on the prison yard. Early morning was cool, almost cold. The only sounds were the scuff of the booted feet of the firing squad, the faint jingle of their accoutrements and the muffled roll of the drums.

It was an eerie sensation, this being marched out to be shot. Royal knew how those seventeen fellow Texans who'd drawn the black beans at Salado had felt. He tried to see Dijon's face and couldn't. The fog was too dense.

Now the main gate lay behind them. Still the muffled drums rolled and scuff of booted feet went on. It wasn't until they reached the northwest corner of the parade ground that *Capitán* Dijon gave the order to halt.

The Frenchman was sarcastically polite as he escorted Royal the few feet to the bullet-pocked outer wall of the prison. 'A tough break for you, Major. Any little last thing I can do?

A cigarillo, perhaps? A blindfold?'

Royal studied his face. 'No, thank you.'

The Frenchman shrugged. 'It's your funeral.'

He turned abruptly and strode back to the line of men. Then he barked an order in Spanish and there was a ragged ripple of rifle bolts.

Royal attempted to draw himself up to attention but every quivering nerve in his body rebelled. The mist was still so thick it formed a chest-high wall of white vapor that hid the six-man rifle unit. But being so tall, he stood head and shoulders above it. The soldiers couldn't miss him if they tried. Not at a scant eighteen feet.

Dijon gave his following commands in Spanish also. 'Ready. Take aim. Fire.'

A volley of shots drowned out the roll of the drums. Royal felt the impacts strike his body and spin him partially around. He didn't have to pretend to fall.

Catana was lying, he thought, and the thought made him a little sad. They could have spared him that last indignity. He lay with his mouth in the dust as the bell in the prison chapel began to toll in answer to the shots. Then a pair of heavy, polished boots materialized through the fog and stopped just short of his head. He felt the cold barrel of a revolver being pressed against his ear.

He sensed Dijon bending over him. 'Not

20

bad, eh, Major?' he whispered in English. 'Your Edwin Booth couldn't have staged it better. Now when I march the squad back to the prison, you get up and run like hell for the clump of trees at the north end of the parade ground.'

The report of the revolver pressed to his ear deafened Royal momentarily. But Catana hadn't been lying. The shot had gone into the ground.

When his hearing returned, the drums were playing a quick step and the scuff of boots was barely audible. Only the bell in the prison chapel continued to toll for his assumed death.

Royal took a deep breath. The whole thing was not a joke. Dijon had been paid off and he'd done a good job of the false execution. The blows that had knocked Royal to the ground had come from heavy paper wads fired from blank cartridges.

He lay a moment longer with his mouth pressed to the dust. Then he got to his feet and in a crouch as low as he could manage, to take advantage of the thinning fog, he ran for the far end of the half-mile-long parade ground.

He was three-quarters of the way when the fog lifted. Unless they, too, had been paid off, which seemed unlikely, one of the sentries on the rampart was bound to see him and sound the alarm. Royal ran on doggedly, expecting to hear a shot any moment.

He could see the waiting horses. He

redoubled his efforts as a man called from the clump of trees, 'Here, Major Royal. Here.'

Breathing in painful gasps, his own sweat blinding him, Royal ran toward the voice. He was less than fifty yards from the trees when the heavy boom of the escape gun sounded. A moment later a bugle blared and glancing back over his shoulder, Royal saw the big gates of the prison open and a troop of soldiers ride out, with *Capitán* Dijon leading them.

Looking back had been a mistake. The troopers were firing as they came. They were not firing blanks this time. A bullet kicked up a spurt of dust inches from Royal's feet. Another flicked his shoulder.

What followed was organized confusion. A horseman, strange to Royal, rode out of the clump of trees, leading a second horse with one hand and firing at the approaching troopers with the heavy-caliber army revolver in his other hand.

'The bastard,' the man swore with feeling. 'The unregenerate renegade louse. He took my money and double-crossed me.'

He reined in his horse and tossed the bridle of the one he was leading to Royal. 'Can you ride?'

Royal gripped the pommel and swung himself up into the saddle. 'I think so.'

'Then don't just sit there like a fool. Get out of here.' Despite the need for haste, the mounted man returned his gun to its holster and slipped a repeating Winchester from the sheath on his saddle and fired with much more effect on the now not so eager troopers. 'I'll cover you for as long as I can, then join you.'

Royal rode for the clump of trees and narrow trail beyond. He had a vague impression of seeing Catana sitting a horse as if she'd been born on one. He thought he saw a fat Mexican who resembled Don Jesus. He knew that his saddle was wet and slippery with blood and that leaves and branches were whipping viciously at his face and shoulders.

But he was alive. Badly wounded or not, he felt more physically alive than he had since the rain-drenched night in Dry Prairie when he'd returned from the war to find a Yankee colonel in his saddle and the black-haired Texas girl who'd sworn to be his loving and faithful wife, obviously enjoying the ride.

CHAPTER FOUR

Cora Royal lay for long moments after awakening without opening her eyes. The large bedroom was comfortably cool. The distant murmuring of the Mexican house servants quietly going about their morning duties to avoid disturbing her was a pleasant sound.

So was the bawling of the trail herd being

readied for the long drive north to Abilene.

She'd gotten the longhorns for nothing. They would cost her perhaps a dollar apiece to gather and road-brand and drive. It was said that Texas cattle were selling for ten to fourteen dollars a head at the railhead. There were thirty-five hundred longhorns in the herd. Allowing for the natural hazards of the trail, she should net a minimum profit of over thirty thousand dollars for the drive. And Kelly would return with the money. She'd made certain of that last night.

She opened her eyes and smiled thinly. She'd come a long way from the adobe in which she'd been born. She was determined to go a lot farther. This money was just the beginning. It would take a lot of money to do what she was planning.

She swung her bare feet to the floor and clapped her hands. Conchita appeared with a cup of coffee for her. As she drank it, she watched in amusement as the girl fluttered about the room, gathering up petticoats and stockings and other intimate wear Cora had discarded the night before.

Men, thank God, especially Texas men, were so impetuous.

She was a little afraid of her new red-haired foreman. But she thought she could handle this man, Kelly. She was sure of it after last night. Men, all men, were such fools. They were all so eager to confuse a woman's heart with other portions of her anatomy.

She ordered breakfast, then dressed, uncertain whether to wear *zapatos* or *botas,* and decided on her new boots. Colonel Simmons didn't approve of the highly polished kid boots trimmed with tassels and decorated with the red star of Texas. He claimed they were identical with those worn by the girls in the tony houses in Abilene. She mentally tossed her head. While she owed a lot to Bill Simmons, he didn't own her. Besides, the boots were comfortable and convenient. A girl couldn't very well wear a gun and holster but she could keep a gun in a boot top.

Breakfast was a leisurely affair. Cora Royal ate it admiring the additions she'd built onto the old Royal ranch house. Her late husband wouldn't approve but it was now more of a fort than a house. The outer walls were four feet thick and twelve feet high, with enough room and stable space to house a regiment of retainers. The hell with what John would have thought. He was dead and she was gambling for big stakes.

She looked up, annoyed, as Hal Mason, one of the men in charge of the newly formed trail herd, galloped into the courtyard and dismounted in front of the open gallery on which she was sitting.

'What is it?' she asked him coldly.

'Trouble,' Mason told her. 'Old man Johnson and two of his boys claim some of their critters have gotten mixed up with our herd.'

'Can't Kelly take care of them?'

The rider nodded. 'Yes, ma'am. But seeing as you gave strict orders not to throw down on any of the locals, Tim thought he'd best send me to ask you what you wanted him to do.'

'I'll come myself,' Cora said.

Mason grinned. 'Yes, ma'am. Tim thought you might want to handle it.'

The trail herd was ready to start. The point and the drag had been posted. The chuck wagons were loaded and their canvas lashed. As Cora rode up she saw her trail boss standing in the center of a group of mounted men. He was talking earnestly to white-haired old Mr. Johnson and his two hulking sons. The old man refused to be placated.

'Don't come that Irish soft soap on me. You people are no better than a passel of thieving Apaches. You know you've got at least four hundred of my critters in that herd.'

Cora reined in her horse. 'What seems to be the trouble, Tim?'

Her trail boss touched the brim of his hat. 'No trouble, Mrs. Royal. Just a misunderstanding. Mr. Johnson here seems to think we have some of his cattle mixed in with ours.'

'Think, nothing,' the old man said. 'It's plain thievery, Mrs. Royal. And if the major had come back from the war, he'd never have

26

stood for it.'

Cora eyed him coldly. She despised old men. They reminded her of her own futile, shiftless father. When she spoke her voice was as cold as her eyes. 'I admire your courage, Mr. Johnson. But speaking of thievery, aren't you being a bit premature?' She gestured with the heavy silver mounted riding crop she affected. 'You say there are four hundred of your cattle in my herd. All right. You tell us which ones are yours and I'll have Mr. Kelly cut them out.'

The younger Johnsons looked at the herd uncertainly. 'That's just it, Mrs. Royal,' their father said. 'We ain't got around to branding all of our increase yet. You know as well as I do that during the war years cattle weren't worth nothing, so we didn't bother. But now that critters are bringing up to fourteen dollars a head at Abilene, your men are sweeping the range clean.'

'Can you prove that?'

'No. But—'

'Go ahead,' the girl challenged him. 'Point out just one animal that belongs to you.'

Old man Johnson was as uncertain as his sons had been. 'Well, take that young bull there. The one with the broken horn. I know danged well he's mine. I've seen him in the draw back of the house a dozen times.'

Cora Royal nodded to two of her mounted men. 'Cut that bull out of the herd and give

27

him to Mr. Johnson. We certainly wouldn't want to profit just because some squatter is too lazy to brand his own cattle.'

Grinning, the riders roped the bull and tried to drag the bawling animal out of the herd while their fellow riders whooped and called encouragement.

His face as red as his neck, Johnson said, 'Now, just one minute, Mrs. Royal. One critter won't do us no good. If you'll only listen to me—'

Cora cut him short. 'No. You listen to me, Mr. Johnson. You talk about thievery. Then you come here and try to cheat a helpless young widow out of four hundred head of her own cattle.' She lifted her riding skirt and took the pearl-handled gun from the top of her boot. 'Well, two can play at that game. Now you and your sons get off my land and take your one-horned bull with you. And if I see you on my ranch again, I'll consider it trespassing and I'll shoot the three of you as quick as I'd shoot an old coyote and his pups.'

To prove that she meant what she said, she fired a shot that missed the old man's boot by a dust spurt. 'I told you to get. Now get!'

The old man stood his ground for a moment, then nodded to his sons and the three men walked stiff-legged to their horses, mounted them and rode away without looking back.

Cora Royal turned to Kelly. 'Now get these

cattle moving. You ought to make at least five miles before you bed down for the night.'

'Whatever you say, Mrs. Royal,' Kelly said. He gave orders to move the herd out, then mounted and rode back toward the house with his employer. 'Know something?' he asked confidentially. 'You're sure one she-devil, honey.'

'You didn't seem to think so last night.'

'That was last night. You knew that old man Johnson would never draw a gun on a woman. That's why you did what you did. And when this gets around Dry Prairie we won't have to steal 'em out. Old man Johnson and his boys will be laughed right out of the county.'

The black-haired girl shrugged. 'Good riddance.'

Kelly asked the question on his mind. 'How about riding back after I bed down the outfit?'

She smiled and shook her head. 'I'd like that. You know that, Tim. I proved that to you last night. But I have to think of my reputation. No. I'm just as sorry about it as you are but we'd better wait until you get back from Abilene.'

'And you won't let that Yankee colonel beat my time?'

'You know better than that.' Cora lost interest in the subject. 'You're certain now there are no King cattle in the drive?'

'Not that I know of.'

'Or Keneny?'

Kelly laughed. 'Or Keneny. Both Dick King and Mifflin Keneny are *muy* tough *hombres* and I'd just as lief keep from tangling with them.'

'How about that Yankee who bought out Big Foot Harper?'

'We may have a few of his mixed in,' Kelly admitted. 'But if we have, they're wearing your brand. Besides, I ain't seen him around for almost four months now. Could be he's pulled out.'

'After paying as much as he did for a forty-thousand-acre grant?'

Kelly guided his horse closer to hers. 'I'd much rather talk about us.'

Cora made certain they weren't being observed, then allowed the trail boss to kiss her. 'Until you get back from Abilene. Now you'd better get back to the drive.'

'Sure, honey. Whatever you say.'

She watched him rejoin the drive starting its nine-hundredmile trek to Kansas, then rode slowly back to the ranch. Being a woman, especially a well-formed, pretty woman, was a decided asset. But it also had its disadvantages. She'd planned the preceding night so that Kelly would be sure to return with the money from the sale of the cattle. But what would she do about him after he'd given her the cash? Men were peculiar creatures. Just because a girl allowed a man to make love to her a night or two, the damned fool thought he owned her.

Bill Simmons, back from his trip to Austin, was waiting for her on the gallery. She hoped the youthful commander of the Union garrison wasn't drinking. She didn't feel like coping with a drunk. She'd cut it too fine, as it was. If Bill had returned a few hours earlier, fur, probably her own, would surely have been flying.

She allowed Manuel to help her dismount, then walked up onto the gallery. 'How nice to see you, Colonel.'

Simmons didn't bother to get to his feet. 'Come off it, Cora. Who do you think we're fooling? All of Dry Prairie knows about us and have for the last three years.'

Cora sat down and fanned herself with his uniform hat. 'You did ride to Austin?'

'I did.'

'And I was right about the agreement under which Texas came into the Union?'

Simmons made a mock salute. 'You were. Talk about legalized blackmail. It's right there on the books. By congressional statute, the only state in the Union so favored, at any time its people desire, they can divide the state of Texas into five separate states having equal power and equal representation with every other state in the country.'

She continued to fan herself. 'Good. Did you talk to any of the boys around the capitol?'

'A few I thought I could trust. And they all

jumped at the idea.'

Cora thought aloud. 'The Sovereign State of Royal. With power to levy taxes and make laws.'

Simmons poured whiskey in his glass. 'With you as Madame Governor? And just what would that make me? The leader of the minority in the House? Or First Lord of the Bedchamber?'

'Don't be vulgar.'

'That's difficult around you.'

Simmons downed his drink. 'There is money in the idea. Possibly millions of dollars. But I'm not sure it doesn't border on treason. And if we do pull this thing off, we'll have to do it before Texas is formally readmitted into the Union.'

'When do you think that will be?'

'Probably late next year. At least that's the last official word I've had.'

'That gives us a year and a half.'

Simmons changed the subject. 'I see you got your herd off.'

'Yes.'

'What was the final tally?'

'Three thousand, four hundred and ninety-nine.'

'Do you think you can trust Kelly to come back with the money?'

Cora couldn't help feeling smug about it. 'I . . . think so.'

It was the wrong tone to take to Simmons

when he'd been drinking. He got to his feet and pulled Cora to hers. 'Now, look here, Cora,' he warned her. 'I've strung along with you for three years. I've risked my commission for you time after time. But if I ever catch you with another man I'll kill you.'

Cora put her hands on his shoulders. 'You know there could never be anyone but you, Bill.' She leaned closer and kissed him. 'There. Does that make you feel any better?'

'Some.'

'Do you want to go into the house?'

Simmons sat back in his chair. 'No, thank you. I can wait until tonight.' He poured more whiskey into his glass.

'Do you have to drink so much?'

'Possibly not, but I'm worried. Face it, Cora. What this really amounts to is secession.'

'You face it,' she countered. 'If we can put this over, we'll own one-fifth of Texas. Think of it, Bill. Thousands and thousands of square miles of some of the richest land in the world. Plus more wild cattle and horses than we can count. Plus salt and coal mines and who knows what else under the surface.'

'I know.' Simmons got to his feet and fitted his hat to his head. 'It's funny, though.'

'What's funny?' Cora asked.

'What a woman can do to a man. Instead of aiding and abetting you, I ought to arrest you for treason.'

Cora put her arms around his neck. 'Now

you know you don't mean that. Would you want me locked up in some federal prison where you wouldn't ever see me again?'

'No. God forgive me, I wouldn't.' Simmons tried, not very strenuously, to remove her arms. 'Now stop kissing me, Cora. Or—'

'Or you'll do what?'

'I will take you into the house.'

'I dare you,' the dark-eyed girl said. 'I dare you.'

An hour later, when Simmons rode away from the ranch, Cora didn't bother to dress. She was too immersed in dreams of the future. What had started as a joke, a vaguely remembered paragraph in one of the books in the one-room school she'd attended, had become a serious matter. What was more, the odds were with her. Once she lighted a fire, it would spread. First one and then another of the larger landholders, she hoped, would take up the clamor to divide Texas into five separate states before it re-entered the Union.

Her overstimulated mind raced on. Texas hadn't been too eager for annexation in the first place. Texans were unique. For the most part they were rough, rugged men who had carved their holdings out of a country as untamed as they were. Men who wanted to live free, on their own terms. Legally constituted authority in any form irked them.

This thing she was planning would take some doing but it could be done. There were still about ten thousand dollars in the Royal account in the bank in Dry Prairie. When Kelly came back with the cattle money she would have thirty thousand more.

She closed her eyes. Now that Bill Simmons had looked in the files and found the statute that gave her a quasi-legal premise to stand on, her first step would be to spend a few thousand dollars to equip her own army. Southeast Texas swarmed with hungry desperadoes, gunfighters and ex-Confederate soldiers who would be pleased to sign up for any cause for a hundred dollars a month and their keep plus a chance to do the federal government a disservice. Between them and Bill's legitimate troops, she could quell any opposition.

When the issue was put to the ballot, she would order the local people to vote. And the *paisanos,* as well as the vaqueros, the small ranch owners and storekeepers, would vote as she wanted them to. So would the saloonkeepers and the gamblers. All she need promise them was that, no matter what laws might be passed in the rest of the former state of Texas, the state of Royal would be wide open.

Her fellow owners of large tracts would be a bigger problem. But they could be handled. Her immediate concern was to keep Tim Kelly and Bill Simmons apart while she was using them to accomplish her purpose. That shouldn't be too difficult. As with their opinions as to the location of a woman's heart, their brains were really not in their heads.

The noon sun was pouring through the window and turning the bedroom into an oven. Hoping it was cooler outside, she put on a light wrapper and walked out onto the gallery, envisioning the future she was planning.

Then, when the new state was an established fact, Simmons and Kelly could go roll their own hoops. She had no intention of marrying either one of them. She was shooting for bigger game.

She took a dipper of water from the red clay jar on the gallery and realized that Manuel was watching her again. The doglike devotion of the aged major-domo annoyed her. It seemed every time she looked up the old man's reproachful eyes were on her. Not that she gave a damn what he or Conchita or any of the help thought.

'Now what's the matter?' she asked him.

The old Mexican spread his hands. 'But nothing, *señora*. I was just wondering, politely, how the *señor* can abide so long away from anyone so beautiful as the *señora*.'

Cora was pleased until she realized what he'd said. 'The *señor*? You're out of your mind, old man. Major Royal is dead. He was killed in the war.'

It pained the old man to disagree with his mistress. 'Ah, but no, gracious *señora*. Dead, perhaps. But not in the war. The Major returned to the *rancho* Royal very much alive. I, myself, saw him with these old eyes. He was standing on the gallery right here one rainy midnight. I saw him looking in through the lighted windows of the *señora's* bedroom.'

Cora dropped the dipper into the jar with a splash. She said, incredulous, 'You saw Major Royal looking through the window of my bedroom?'

'*Sí, señora.*' The old man beamed. 'But as I did not wish to intrude on so happy a reunion, I walked away without speaking.' He shook his head. 'And the next morning I was *muy* sad when the Major did not come out to greet all of us who love him.' He sighed. 'But I am an old man and not very smart and I do not know the reason for many things.'

'Are you absolutely sure it was the Major?'

'*Sí, señora.*'

'What night was this, Manuel? Think hard.'

Manuel tried to remember. 'It was long ago, gracious *señora. Uno, dos, tres* years ago.' His face brightened. 'It was on a *sábado noches,* right after the war. On the night of the big fiesta in Dry Prairie. On the night it rained so hard but none of us cared because we were all drunk and so happy that the war was over.'

Cora leaned against one of the posts that supported the roof of the gallery. On the night of the big fiesta in Dry Prairie. That would have been the night she'd first met Bill

Simmons and because it had been raining so hard, he'd insisted on driving her home from the dance that the new Union garrison had given. Her cheeks felt flushed. As she remembered, they'd both been more than slightly high and after they'd reached the ranch, one thing had led to another. And if John Royal had chosen that night to come home and look through the windows of her bedroom he'd seen plenty.

It wasn't fair. John couldn't be alive. He had to be dead. 'Why didn't you tell me this before?' she demanded.

Manuel was hurt at her tone. 'You never asked me, *señora.*'

Cora chose her words carefully. 'Did any of the other servants see him?'

The major-domo shrugged. 'I do not know. But if they did, none of them remarked it to me. And in the morning the major's horse was gone.'

Cora breathed a little more easily. Riding away was the sort of thing a quixotic fool like John Royal would do. She wet her lips with the tip of her tongue. 'And how many people did you tell?'

'No one, *señora.*' He amended the statement. 'Just the one *yanqui procurador* who they say paid much in gold for the *rancho* and cattle of *Señor* Big Foot Harper.'

Cora considered the information. She could take care of the Yankee fool who'd bought the

Harper spread. But John was another matter. If Manuel was telling the truth, if Royal was still alive, he could upset all her plans.

CHAPTER FIVE

Royal was cold. Every time he breathed he coughed. As near as he could tell, he was lying on a Cherokee bed, sleeping on his stomach and his only cover was his stern.

He pushed himself to a sitting position. He was in a rock cave of some kind. That much was obvious. It was the thin smoke from a small cooking fire that was making him cough. Catana was kneeling on the far side of the fire, intent on stirring something in a little pot made of heavy iron.

He started to speak to her but caught himself as a fat Mexican entered the cave. He'd been right in thinking he'd seen Don Jesus in the clump of trees at the far end of the parade ground. Now, moving with surprising speed for such a fat man, the cantina owner motioned for the girl to remove her pot from the fire, then scattered the burning twigs with his booted feet and returned to the mouth of the cave and stood in an attitude of listening, with his rifle clutched in one pudgy hand.

The girl listened with him for a moment. Then, seeing that Royal was awake and sitting up, she brought the pot over to where he was and began to spoon gruel into his mouth.

Royal tried to protest but he was too weak to say a word. He managed to swallow one spoonful, and another and another, until the little pot was empty.

'Where—?' he managed to whisper but stopped short as Catana put a finger to her lips.

She looked different. He realized why. The first time he'd seen her in the Golden Rooster, with a black silk mantilla over her wheat-colored hair, she'd been dressed as a *señorita* of breeding. When she'd visited him in his cell, with her blond hair dyed black, she'd looked like a cantina girl. Now wearing a pair of vaquero pants and a blue wool shirt a few sizes too large, her still-black waist-long hair cropped close to her head and a smudge of charcoal on her nose, she looked like a boy. A very soft and pretty boy.

As Royal, puzzled, studied her face, a second man came in. 'It's all right,' he informed Don Jesus. 'They didn't spot us. But it's a good thing we had the horses under cover.'

Royal looked from the girl to the man. He was a big man, tall and soft spoken. He looked like the man who'd asked him if he could ride, then stayed behind to cover his escape.

'He is awake,' Catana told him. She looked back at Royal and added, 'And I think he's much better.'

The newcomer was pleased. 'Good. We can use another gun.' He squatted down beside Royal. 'How are you feeling, fellow?'

'Weak,' Royal admitted.

The other man offered his hand. 'The name is Tyler. Jim Tyler.'

Don Jesus joined them. 'Is *yanqui procurador* who was asking for you in San Rosario.'

'Oh,' Royal said. He inched his back against the rock and sat a little straighter. 'Now, would one of you please tell me what this is all about and where we are?'

Tyler shifted the crossed gunbelts he was wearing. 'I don't rightly know the name of this particular range. But I imagine it's a part of the Sierra Madres. Judging by the distance we've traveled we should be well into the state of Chihuahua.'

Royal mulled over the information. It was a hard week's ride from San Rosario to the nearest point in Chihuahua and after one left the coast all of it was rough going. But he'd escaped prison just this morning! He protested, 'But that's impossible.'

Tyler smiled thinly. 'No. We've done it. But I'll tell you something, Major. After watching you ride these past two weeks with that hole in your shoulder and with no medical attention, I'm beginning to wonder how we ever whipped you fellows.'

41

Royal asked, incredulous, 'You mean that it's been two weeks since the morning of that faked firing squad?'

'That's right. And you rode every foot of the way.'

'Unconscious?'

'No. You were conscious but out of your mind. You refought every battle you'd been in.' Tyler's grin widened. 'That is, when you weren't bellowing that little ditty about "Jeff Davis built a wagon and on it put a name, and Beauregard was driver and Secession was the same."'

Royal touched the crude bandage on his shoulder.

Tyler went on, 'Then two days ago you came to the end of your strength and we holed up here until you get strong enough to go on.'

'And we're still being followed?'

Tyler nodded, 'That's right. That was Dijon and his men who just went by.'

'But I thought he sold out to you.'

'He did. Then double-crossed me to put on a show for the friends of that colonel you killed. They must have laughed fit to split their coffee-colored hides when you picked yourself up and ran. Now I imagine he's in trouble with the big brass in Mexico City and that's why he's trying so hard to stop you before you can get across the border.'

'I see,' Royal said. He looked at Catana, then at Don Jesus. 'But what are they doing

42

here?'

Tyler sighed. 'I didn't plan it this way, believe me. But after things went as wrong with the escape as they did, they couldn't very well stay in San Rosario. The authorities would have stood Don Jesus against a wall. And you know what would have happened to Catana.'

'Yes,' Royal said. 'I know.'

He looked at Catana. She met his eyes for a moment, then got to her feet and began to rebuild the scattered fire. There was more, a lot more to her part of this than he knew. While she certainly hadn't been a virgin when she'd given herself to him in his cell, neither had she been a cantina girl. She had the air and the breeding of a lady. He might never know why she'd been so kind.

Don Jesus added more twigs to the fire she'd relighted. The warmth felt good.

Royal tried to think of something to say. He said, 'Judging from the cold, we must be fairly high.'

Don Jesus attempted to warm his hands over the small flame. '*Sí, señor.* Very high.'

Royal continued, 'Saying thank you seems very inadequate. I must have been quite a problem to all of you.'

Don Jesus shrugged. Catana added more twigs to the fire. Tyler said, 'You'll get a bill in due time.' He took a piece of jerked meat from his pocket and gave it to Royal. 'But right now, chew on this. The sooner you get strong enough to ride again the better off we'll all be.'

Royal chewed on the jerky. 'What did I talk about these last two weeks?' he asked.

'The war,' Tyler answered. 'Texas. Your ranch. Things you'd done when you were a boy. The medical school you went to. Cantina girls who insisted on having babies in the middle of the night.' Tyler smiled his quick smile. 'If Catana will excuse the expression, you claimed that during these past three years you delivered more bastards than made that walk with Sherman.'

Royal was relieved that he hadn't talked about Cora. He'd made a big enough fool of himself as it was. He still didn't know why they'd interested themselves in him but he did know he owed Tyler and Catana and Don Jesus more than he could ever repay.

Tyler stood up and made sure his guns slid easily in their holsters. 'I'd better have a last look around before we bed down for the night.' He nodded to Don Jesus. 'And while I'm gone you'd better pull some more bunch grass for the horses. If the major thinks he can manage it, we'd better ride out of here tomorrow.'

'*Sí*,' the fat man agreed.

Tyler added, 'And now that you're in your right mind, Major, you can begin to pull your share of the load.' He indicated a narrow passage in the cave. 'You'll find a .44 and a

44

gunbelt back there with the horses and saddlebags. I was afraid to let you wear them before.'

Royal got to his feet with some effort. His legs felt a little unstable but he could walk after a fashion. He found the gun and gunbelt and he felt much better after he'd buckled the belt. When he returned to the cave, Catana was still crouching before the fire.

'Why?' Royal asked her.

The girl ignored the question. 'Perhaps you should not move around so freely.'

Royal squatted beside her and spread his palms over the flame. 'I feel all right. Just a little weak, that's all. I asked you a question, Catana.'

'And I don't want to talk about it.'

'All right,' Royal said.

He unbuttoned his shirt and peered under the bandage on his left shoulder. Whoever had treated the wound had done a good job. The mouth was puckering nicely.

'I imagine you did this.'

'Yes,' the girl said, 'I did.'

'You did a good job.'

'*Gracias.*' Catana was apologetic. 'It was the first time I'd ever treated a wound and I do not know much about such things but I changed and washed the bandage every day.'

'Where did you get the linen?'

Her voice was small as it had been on the afternoon in his cell. 'I used my *camisilla* and

45

my petticoats.'

Royal glanced sideways at her. Now that he was getting used to it, he liked her cropped hair. It didn't really make her look like a boy. Nothing could do that. Even in vaquero pants and the too large wool shirt she was completely feminine and one of the most beautiful girls he'd ever seen.

Don Jesus, panting from his exertions in the thin air, returned with an armful of bunch grass and after they'd spread it before the horses, Royal insisted on helping him gather more.

Shortly before sunset Tyler came in with a brace of quail he'd stunned with stones and a young kid he'd killed with his knife. There was enough meat for a feast but it was too close to sundown to cook it. As high in the mountains as they were, even the glimmer of a fire would be visible for miles. There was no doubt about it. If they managed to reach the border, all the credit would belong to Tyler. This tall stranger not only knew his business, he was a master forager. He knew how to live off the land.

Supper was a simple but ample meal of cold tortillas and frijoles that Catana had cooked earlier in the day. While they ate, Tyler assigned the watches. Don Jesus would take the first and he the second. Royal demanded a watch and was told curtly, by Tyler, that the most important thing he could do for the general welfare was to conserve and rebuild his strength so they could push on as rapidly as possible.

Then, with the small fire extinguished as soon as darkness had fallen and a thin bed of grass spread on the warm stones for Catana, Tyler and Royal tried to sleep.

The heat from the extinct fire soon faded. It was very cold in the cave. Royal knew he should be uncomfortable but he wasn't. In spite of the dull ache in the healing wound, he felt fine. For the first time in three years, his head was clear of tequila and aguardiente fumes and his mind was no longer sodden with self-pity. He realized he felt better than he'd felt since the morning he'd ridden out of Dry Prairie in the fall of 1861.

He lay staring up into the dark, wondering, if they did make it, if they could elude Captain Dijon and his men and manage to cross the border, how much of his life he could salvage. That situation wasn't entirely hopeless. He still had his profession and his ranch. He could make some sort of a deal with Cora, give her half the ranch if he had to.

Catana's rhythmic breathing was a pleasant and homey sound. He liked Tyler. He liked him very much. The girl had gone to sleep almost immediately but he didn't think Tyler had.

'Are you asleep, Tyler?' he asked.
'Not yet.'
'Thanks for getting me out of San Rosario.'

'I had a reason.'

'I figured that. Mind telling me what it is?'

Tyler was silent a few minutes. 'That's a long story, Major. For now, let's just say I figure you're much more valuable to me alive than you would be back there rotting in an unmarked prison grave.'

'You aren't on official business? It's not something to do with the government?'

'God, no,' the other man said emphatically. 'The war has been over for three years. But how about letting it rest until we get to know each other a little better?'

'Whatever you say,' Royal answered him. He thought a moment, then added, 'But I would appreciate it if you would tell me this much. After we cross the border, if we do, have you any particular destination in mind?'

'Yes. Dry Prairie, Texas.'

'You have interests there?'

'I suppose you might say I have. I used all my army pay and a lot more that I'd saved before that, to buy out Big Foot Harper's spread. Lock, stock, barrel, and cactus.'

'The ranch next to mine?'

'That's right.'

'Then you know my wife?'

'We've met.'

Tyler left it there. Royal didn't pursue the subject. The other man would talk when he was ready. He changed the subject. 'You know, you're pretty good at living off the land. You must have ridden with Stuart, or was it Early?'

Tyler sounded as if he were trying not to laugh. 'Well, no, not exactly. It so happens I'm one of those bastards who made that little walk with Sherman.'

CHAPTER SIX

The wheels of the carriage were painted a Chinese red. The black patent-leather upper body glistened in the sun. The thick white cord fringe along the four sides of the top swung rhythmically with the sway of the horses. To the best of Cora Royal's knowledge, it was the only carriage of its kind south of New Orleans and north of Mexico City. At least so the buggy salesman who'd sold it to her had claimed. What was more, it was called a surrey, because it had been built in England in a town of that name.

It had cost plenty, she reflected, but it was worth the money she'd spent. It wouldn't be long before everyone in South Texas, in all of the adjoining states, for that matter, knew who Cora Royal was. And, after all, she had to live up to her new social status.

Cora rode with her full skirt and petticoats spread in the same genteel fashion she'd seen in the etching in the most recent edition of *Godey's Lady's Book.* She wished the old hags on the Brazos could see her now. Ike Hooper's black-haired daughter had come a long way from the one-room adobe in which she'd been born. In the three and a half months since she'd put her plan into operation, she hadn't encountered one serious obstacle. Once it had become known that she was hiring, she'd had her pick of the choicest cutthroats from Nacogdoches to Brownsville. There was only one small fly in her barrel of molasses.

Cora studied the red-haired rider through slitted eyes. Ever since his return from Abilene with the money for the trail herd, Kelly had become embarrassingly possessive. It was getting more difficult every day to keep him and Simmons apart. Just because she'd granted the man a few favors, the barrel-chested trail boss thought he owned her.

Definitely, she had to do something about Kelly, and soon.

He urged his horse up beside the surrey and grinned. 'Well, today should teach the die-hards who's boss.'

'Yes,' Cora agreed, 'it should.'

'I told you old man Johnson was a troublemaker. You should have let me take care of him that day I started the herd for Abilene.'

'It's better this way.'

'Maybe so.'

As the surrey and the flanking riders crossed the wood planking over waterless

Gilmore Creek, Cora sat back on the seat and studied the wooden false fronts and adobes lining the street. At least the local merchants should be on her side. Since she'd started to beat the drum to put the division of Texas to a vote, the population of Dry Prairie had doubled, then tripled, then quadrupled.

Adventurers and salesmen, would-be office holders and favor seekers, gamblers and fancy women had swarmed into the town like so many ants attracted by the frosting on a cake. Besides, from the bits of information she'd picked up here and there, the fire she'd lighted was spreading. Not that she gave a tinker's dam what happened to the rest of Texas. All she was interested in was her own one-fifth of the state. Bill Simmons had already begun to call her 'Madame Governor.' In jest, of course. She patted her hair under her smart new bonnet. But it might not be in jest forever.

Kelly brought his horse up beside the surrey again. 'Do you want to stop at the bank?'

'No,' Cora said. 'I don't trust Kirby.'

She didn't. She hadn't trusted Mr. Kirby since he'd given her that funny look on the day she'd withdrawn the entire ten thousand dollars from her and John Royal's joint account. Any money she collected from now on, including the thirty-odd thousand dollars that Tim had brought back from Abilene, was safer in the strongbox at the ranch.

Just in case. Not that she'd told Tim or Bill

what Manuel had told her about John. Men were funny that way. There was a basic streak of decency in even the worst of them. It seemed it was one thing to take a young widow to bed, but quite another to make love to another man's wife.

Cora pondered the conversation with the aged major-domo. Even if Manuel had been telling the truth about seeing John Royal, it had been over three years ago. John had to be dead now. If he weren't, he would have returned to Dry Prairie. No man in his right mind would ride away and leave one of the largest ranches in Texas and a juicy bank account just because he happened to come home at an inopportune moment.

No man but John Royal. Any other man would have killed her and Bill Simmons and there wasn't a jury in Texas that would have convicted him.

Cora was smugly amused. Not that it made any difference now. If Royal did come back again, she'd arranged things so he couldn't touch either her or the ranch. The ranch was legally hers. She'd seen to that, with some help from Bill.

She rode, eying the activities on the raised wooden walks. Music blared or tinkled from every third store front. Contrasting with the sober-faced ranchers and riders, sodden drunks staggered in and out of the saloons while over their heads soft-eyed Mexican girls and hard-eyed bleached blondes from points east called out their wares from second-floor windows and openly sneered at the primly dressed ranch and farm wives on the walks.

'Not much like an old court day, is it?' Kelly asked.

'No,' Cora admitted, 'it isn't.' She laid a hand on his arm. 'Please, Tim. For my sake. Take another herd to Abilene. With fifty men on my payroll I need the money. How long do you think thirty thousand dollars will last?'

Kelly was impatient with her. 'Please. Let's not start that again, Cora. I tell you it's too late in the year. We'd run into bad weather before we crossed the Big Red.'

'Don't tell me you're afraid of a little weather.'

'No,' Kelly assured her. 'I'm not afraid. I'm not afraid of anything or anyone. Not even a certain Union colonel. I thought you promised there wouldn't be any hanky panky while I was gone.'

Cora looked at him with wide-eyed innocence. 'You have a dirty mind, Tim Kelly. I don't know what you're talking about.'

'Then why is Colonel Simmons so willing to help you get old man Johnson off our backs? Why did he run Milam and Smith and Fannin out of the county?'

'Because, as the officer in charge of the local Union garrison, it's his sworn duty to preserve the peace.'

'I'll bet. I'll just bet,' Kelly said. 'But don't let me catch you at it, Cora. I killed plenty of blue-bellies in the war and one more won't matter. Not even if he is a colonel.'

Cora sat back on the seat again. Someone, probably Conchita, had been talking to Kelly. She really had to do something about him. Bill Simmons was more important to her than just another gun. She could always find a new foreman and trail boss. Any one of the fifty men she'd hired would be glad to take Kelly's job.

Manuel reined in his team in front of the Dry Prairie county courthouse and Kelly swung down from his horse and helped Cora alight.

'What do you think Simmons will do with Johnson?'

'I haven't any idea.'

'You haven't discussed it with the colonel?'

'Of course not.'

'Then what do you talk about when you and the colonel are together?'

'Now you're being insulting.'

'I'm beginning to wonder.'

'Wonder what?'

'Just how a man could insult you.'

Cora allowed the remark to pass. Whatever she decided to do about Kelly she would have to be clever about it. Kelly was well liked by his men.

The outriders reined in their horses beside

the surrey and Hal Mason, Kelly's second in command, asked, 'Is it all right for the boys to get a drink? Or do you want us to stay around?'

'You'd better stay around,' Kelly said. 'Johnson is a tough old rooster. He may try to make trouble.'

Two Union soldiers were guarding the doorway of the courtroom. There were more Union soldiers in the hall and a platoon of them leaning against the inner wall of the courtroom. Most of the seats were taken. The men sitting in them were farmers and small ranchers. Most of the women were wives of local storekeepers and professional men. They greeted Cora pleasantly and admired the new gown she'd had Jules of New Orleans send down by the Brownsville packet.

As they took the last two available seats, Cora whispered to Kelly, 'The cats. They're so green-eyed with jealousy they'd like to strip me naked if they dared. But they don't. They know who's putting the jam on their johnny bread.'

Cora settled herself in her chair and looked around the room with interest. Wearing full dress uniform and flanked by two heavily armed Union sergeants, Bill Simmons was seated behind the desk that served as a judicial bench, talking earnestly to Pete Watkins, the fat scallawag prosecutor. Old man Johnson and his two sons were seated in the first row.

All three were wearing guns. Johnson's neck was redder than usual.

It was hot in the small courtroom. Cora was glad she'd remembered to bring her smelling salts. She was relieved when one of the Union sergeants, acting as clerk of the court, banged a gavel and announced:

'The United States Military District Court of Dry Prairie, Texas, Colonel William Simmons presiding, is officially convened.'

There was a shuffling of feet and a scraping of chairs but no one bothered to rise.

The sergeant read from a paper that Watkins handed him. 'The United States versus Orin Johnson, charged with conspiracy to incite riot against the properly constituted authority. The defendant will please rise and come forward to the judge's bench.'

Johnson got to his feet and came forward. His two sons hesitated a minute and then followed their father and stood beside him.

'You are Orin Johnson?' Colonel Simmons asked him.

'Yes, sir.'

'You heard the charges against you?'

'I did.'

'How do you plead, guilty or not guilty?'

'Not guilty.' The old man added, earnestly, 'I never incited no one to riot, Colonel. All I done was say around that the Royal woman is a danged thief and if some of us small ranchers don't band together and do something to stop her, her and them hired gunfighters of hers are going to thieve us small fellers clean out of the county.'

There was a loud murmur of voices, some in agreement, some in protest.

Colonel Simmons banged his desk with the gavel. 'The spectators will maintain order in respect for the court. If there is another disturbance of this kind, I will be obliged to ask the sergeants of the guard to clear the room.'

When the room was quiet, Watkins said, 'In my role of prosecutor, may I remind the defendant that Mrs. Royal is not on trial here. You are on trial. If you think you have a just grievance, why didn't you appeal to the law?'

Johnson stood his ground. 'Because there ain't no law.'

'Oh?' Colonel Simmons said. 'What do you call this court?'

'A danged drumhead court-martial, that's what.'

'You are using military terminology.'

'I was in the Army.'

'In the Union Army, I presume?'

Johnson squared his shoulders. 'No, sir. I was with Beauregard at Shiloh. Elijah, here, was with Hood. And my t'other boy rode with Jeb Stuart.'

'In other words, you are all natural-born troublemakers. You all rebelled against your government.'

'We sided with Texas,' Johnson said. Then he added hotly, 'And there's another thing. The way I see it, the only reason Mrs. Royal is pumping for Texas to be divided into five separate states is because she's plumb greedy and she ain't satisfied with what she can steal. She wants us to go to the polls and make it legal. And I been talking against that, too. That's why I got the boys together at my place.'

'You admit you held a meeting at your ranch?'

'I cain't deny it.'

'What was the purpose of this meeting?'

'I was trying to get the boys to form a group of regulators or a vigilante committee.'

'Then you also admit in addition to conspiracy to incite riot, you are guilty of unlawful assembly?'

'I don't know nothing about that. I just know I got the boys together.'

'And urged them to take the law in their own hands.'

'Yes, sir. That's just what I done. I never incited to riot. All I did was say if the Royal woman wanted war, we should give it to her before she burned her RX brand on one-fifth of Texas.'

Colonel Simmons shook his head. 'I'm very much afraid, Mr. Johnson, that by your own words you stand convicted of the charge against you. Have you anything to say before sentence is passed by the court?'

Johnson glowered at the platoon of soldiers lining the walls of the room. 'Get them danged soldiers out of here so me and my boys can have a fair shake and I'll say plenty more.'

'I'm afraid you've already said too much,' Simmons said. 'By the authority vested in me I could sentence you to a long term of imprisonment. But taking your age into consideration, I'm going to be lenient with you, Mr. Johnson. I'll give you exactly twenty-four hours to pack your personal belongings and get out of my jurisdiction.'

Cora squeezed Kelly's arm and whispered, 'See? What did I tell you? Another troublemaker out of the way.'

Johnson was incredulous. 'You mean just ride away and leave my spread?'

'That is exactly what I mean.'

'But you can't take my land away from me. There's no law says you can.'

Colonel Simmons was patient with him. 'I'm not taking anything away from you, Mr. Johnson. I'm merely attempting to preserve the peace.' He glanced at one of the soldiers. 'Sergeant Bryant, escort this man out of my court. And when you get him outside, detail a detachment of troops to accompany him to his ranch. There they will allow him to load two wagons with anything he may desire to take with him. They will then escort him as far as the north bank of the Brazos River. If he tries to break or return, you will order your men to shoot him.'

'Yes, sir,' the sergeant replied.

The eldest Johnson son said, 'But they can't do this to you, Pa.'

Johnson's shoulders sagged. 'They done it.'

Sergeant Bryant reached for his arm and Johnson pulled it away.

'Keepen your hands off me. When I ain't on a horse, I bin walking for sixty years. I guess I still know how.'

There was an embarrassed silence in the courtroom as the old man and his sons slowly walked out, followed by the detachment of soldiers. Colonel Simmons said something to his clerk and the clerk recessed court for fifteen minutes. Simmons rose to his feet and walked into the small room that served as a chamber.

Cora excused herself to Kelly and followed Simmons into the anteroom.

'Nice going, Bill.'

Simmons poured some whiskey into a glass and drank it at one gulp. 'I don't feel nice about it. Blackstone would turn over in his grave if he heard me. That farce out there had no more resemblance to a trial than a prickly pear has to an apple. God help me if General Sheridan ever finds out how I'm running this district. They'll cut off my buttons and drum me out of the Army.'

Cora kissed him. 'That's possible. But look

at all you're gaining.'

Simmons didn't respond to her caress. 'Sometimes I wonder.'

Cora kissed him again and walked out of the room and down the hallway to the door of the courthouse. Kelly was waiting for her outside.

'What did you have to talk to the colonel about?'

Cora looked searchingly into Kelly's face. But he had no expression at all. She thought, He's got to go soon. Jealous men were dangerous.

'The trial,' she said casually.

'Some trial.'

'It got rid of Johnson.'

'He hasn't gone very far.'

Cora looked in the direction in which Kelly's eyes were turned. Completely ignoring Sergeant Bryant and his men, Johnson was at the center of a group of angry men, small ranchers and farmers who'd followed him out of the courtroom.

Cora wet her lips with her tongue. 'If there should be any trouble, let me handle it.'

'You know something, Cora?' Kelly told her. 'One of these days you're going to lean too heavily on the fact that you're a woman and find yourself in a lot of trouble.'

The black-haired girl shrugged. 'Perhaps.'

She started to walk toward her surrey and outriders. Old man Johnson detached himself from the knot of men in front of the courthouse to intercept her.

'Just a minute, Mrs. Royal.'

Cora looked at him with contempt. 'Yes?'

Johnson stood with his feet spread, his gnarled thumbs hooked in his gunbelt. 'I give you credit,' he said. 'You done what you boasted you'd do. You got me and my boys run out of the county. You know danged well we cain't fight the whole Union Army. But I kin fight your pimp and I aim to. Okay, Kelly. Go for your guns. Seeing as how I was born in Texas, I might as well die here.'

The back of Kelly's neck turned a dull brick red. 'Well,' he whispered to Cora. 'If you're going to do something, do it.'

Cora smiled up at him sweetly. 'Why should I? I believe he's talking to you.'

'Draw or crawl, Kelly,' the old man said. 'This time it seems that your fancy skirt has left the play up to you.' The group in front of the courthouse gave them room. Only Cora stayed where she was.

'Well,' she asked Kelly, 'are you a man or aren't you? Or don't you care what he says about me?'

Johnson was old but he was fast. The impact of the bullets spun Kelly around. His drawn gun fell from his hand. He stood a moment, weaving, then followed his gun into the dust. Cora picked up her skirts daintily and stepped over him to continue on her way to her surrey, smiling.

'I'm afraid you're in real trouble now, Mr. Johnson. Serious trouble. You should have left Dry Prairie while you had a chance.'

Johnson's two sons came forward to stand beside their father. The soldiers waited for orders. When Cora reached her surrey, Hal Mason leaned forward in his saddle and looked at her expectantly.

She shook her head. 'Of course not, Hal. Let the law take care of Mr. Johnson. After all, that's what the law is for.'

Attracted by the shots, Colonel Simmons came onto the portico of the courthouse. 'Now what?'

Cora allowed one of her dismounted men to assist her into the surrey. 'I'm very much afraid,' she told Simmons, 'that Mr. Johnson has just killed Mr. Kelly.'

CHAPTER SEVEN

'Arrest those men,' Simmons said.

'The three of them?' Sergeant Bryant asked.

'The three of them.'

Old man Johnson and his sons looked around them to see if they had any support. They didn't. The men to whom they'd been talking a moment before had backed away.

Johnson reversed his gun and handed it to the sergeant. 'Anyway, I got Kelly.'

Cora nodded to Manuel. 'Drive on.'

Her corset was binding her. She could still hear the impact of the three slugs striking Kelly's body. She would never forget the shocked look on his face. Still, when one was founding an empire, one had to expect some unpleasant happenings. It really wasn't her fault. If Kelly hadn't been so possessive and jealous of Bill Simmons, instead of lying dead across his horse, he would be well on his way to Abilene with another profitable trail herd.

She looked up, annoyed, as Manuel halted the team on the town side of the bridge and Hal Mason rode back to the surrey.

'Why have we stopped?' Cora asked him.

Mason took off his hat. 'There's a rider who wants to talk to you, Mrs. Royal. He says when he came through Goliad he heard you were hiring.'

'What's his name?'

'He didn't say.' Mason turned in his saddle and pointed. 'That's him there by the bridge.'

Cora studied the man with interest. A large number of her men had come to her in various degrees of poverty but this one topped them all. If he'd had a hat he'd lost it. He was wearing what looked like a uniform shirt with the insignia ripped off. Pieces of red braid were still visible along the seams of his dusty dark blue trousers. His face was burned black with the sun. He carried himself well and was darkly handsome in a strange, foreign way.

The black-haired girl said thoughtfully, 'He looks like an army man.'

Mason laughed. 'Mexican Army, I'd say. Probably a deserter.'

'Tell him I'll talk to him.'

Cora continued to study the man as he rode up to the surrey. He sat his horse well. He looked like he might know how to use a gun. With Kelly dead, she could use another rider. He might even make a good trail boss. And this time there would be nothing personal in their relationship.

As the rider reined his horse beside the surrey, she said, 'Mr. Mason says you'd like to work for me.'

The man bowed in his saddle. There was a trace of an accent when he spoke. 'That is correct, madame. When I rode through Goliad, I heard you were engaging riders and . . .' The rider left it there as he ran one finger along his wisp of a mustache.

'You seem to have had some bad luck.'

His shrug was emphatic. 'That is as good a name for it as any.'

'I imagine you're broke.'

'Shall we say that I am without funds at the moment?'

'That looks like part of a uniform.'

'Madame is very observant.'

'Enlisted man or officer?'

'Officer.'

'I judged that from your bearing. And from

what is left of your uniform, I'd say you did your soldiering in the Mexican Army.'

'At least recently.'

'You are a deserter?'

'For a very excellent reason.'

She waved the subject aside as immaterial. 'I assume you can use that gun you're wearing?'

There was another suggestion of a bow. 'With facility, madame.'

'And take orders?'

'You will have no reason to question my loyalty.'

Cora studied the man some more. He both attracted and repelled her. He was handsome, but there was something incredibly evil about him. Still, she wasn't running a one-room school for children. She had a long, hard fight before her. It would take men without conscience or scruples to do the things they would be called upon to do. 'All right. I'll take a chance on you. I pay one hundred dollars and board. And you do what you're told to do without question.'

'Without question.'

'Now, just one more thing.'

'*Oui,* madame.'

'You aren't Mexican, are you?'

'No, madame.'

Cora had a distinct impression that if the man hadn't been mounted she would have heard the click of his heels. 'Then what and

66

who are you?'

'I am French, madame. Captain Marcel Dijon, late of the ill-fated *Légion étrangère*. More recently *comandante* of the Mexican federal prison at San Rosario.'

'And still you are willing to work for me for one hundred dollars a month and your keep?'

'I am.'

'Why?'

'You are Mrs. John Royal, are you not?'

'I am Major John Royal's widow.'

The mounted man smiled thinly. 'But no, madame. If you will permit a slight correction, Major John Royal is not dead.'

Cora looked around quickly to see whether anyone had heard him. It seemed no one had. They were all sitting their horses, talking in low tones, waiting for her to give the signal for the cavalcade to continue.

It was difficult for her to ask the question. 'You are certain of this, Dijon?'

'I saw him within the week.'

'Where?'

'At the Favor ranch in the Big Bend country.'

'John was alone?'

'But no, madame. He is with an American named Tyler, a very pretty dark-haired girl and a Mexican national by the name of Don Jesus.'

'You're sure of this?'

Dijon permitted himself another of his thin smiles. 'I couldn't be more positive. You see

Major Royal escaped from a firing squad in San Rosario and I have just spent the last several months pursuing him across half of Mexico, only to have him escape me by crossing the border and finding sanctuary in this country.'

Cora was puzzled. 'Then you are here on official business?'

'No, Mrs. Royal. This affair between Major Royal and myself is strictly personal.'

She liked the way he'd said it. 'You think he's headed this way?'

'That's why I rode on ahead.'

'I believe you mentioned a firing squad.'

'That is correct, madame.'

'And a Mexican girl?'

'That, too, is correct.'

'Very pretty?'

'Very pretty and very young.'

Cora tapped her driver on the shoulder with her crop. 'Drive on, Manuel.' She turned to Dijon. 'You ride beside the surrey, Captain. If I'm correct, and I'm seldom wrong, you and I have a lot in common that I would like to discuss with you.'

CHAPTER EIGHT

It was early evening and there was a full moon in the sky and the smell of green, growing

68

things in the air when Royal returned to Dry Prairie for the second time in eight years. Although it was dry most of the time, a lot of water had flowed under the loose planking over Gilmore Creek.

As Royal rode down the boisterous main street, hock-deep in dust and teeming with riders and buckboards and wagons and a few buggies, he couldn't decide whether or not he was pleased to be home. If all that Tyler and Milt Favor had told him was true, the next few days wouldn't be pleasant ones. No man enjoys watching an old love die.

'Recognize the place?' Tyler asked.

'Barely,' Royal said.

He studied the raised walks on both sides of the street as he rode. The street was unnaturally bright with coal-oil flambeaus attached to the fronts of the buildings. The walks were crowded with drunken soldiers and civilians. Loudmouthed shills stood in front of many of the saloons, capping for roulette wheels and faro banks. Scantily clad girls sat on the sills or leaned out the second-story windows. The clean smell of green, growing things was gone. All he could smell now was whiskey, cheap perfume and greasy meat frying.

Tyler urged his horse up beside Royal's. 'Are you going to ride out to the ranch tonight?'

'No,' Royal said. 'I think I'll postpone that

until morning. For one thing, I want to stop at the bank and get some money.' He glanced over his shoulder to be sure that Catana and Don Jesus were behind them. 'For another, I still don't know what I'm going to do about Catana.'

'You know you're all welcome at my place.'

'I know. But you've done enough for me. It's about time I began to stand on my own two feet.'

'In that case,' Tyler said drily, 'I think I'll stay in town, too.'

'After being away from your spread as long as you have?'

Tyler shrugged. 'That's a nice thing about owning acreage. A man may lose a few hundred head of cattle but no one can trail herd his land to Abilene.'

Royal dismounted in front of the Commercial Hotel and tied his mount to the hitchrack. The coming scene with Cora was bound to be a nasty one. Naturally, she would deny any improper conduct. He couldn't prove what he'd seen. She would probably accuse him of having deserted her.

Now, three years later, he could be in for trouble. A dozen men in Goliad had confirmed what Favor had told him. During the last few months Cora had not only fortified the ranch, she'd engaged a small army of gunmen. As the story went, she had the commander of the local garrison in her reticule or, more properly, under her bustle. Favor had told them that between Cora and Colonel Simmons and a trail boss named Kelly, they ran Dry Prairie and the surrounding countryside to suit themselves.

More, the issue of dividing Texas into five separate states had earned his wife and her hangers-on a hard core of unpaid sympathizers and adherents composed of saloon men, gamblers, pimps and greedy storekeepers.

Don Jesus was pleased with the music and the activities on the walks. 'Is just like San Rosario in fiesta,' he beamed.

Royal helped Catana from her horse. 'I imagine you're tired.'

'*Sí*,' the girl said without expression.

Standing beside him, she barely reached to his chin. In the flickering light of the flaming flambeaus the blond roots of her hair were clearly visible under the strands of her dyed hair. One of the first things he had to do, Royal thought, was get the girl some decent clothes. She couldn't spend the rest of her life in vaquero pants and a man's wool shirt. But even when he'd restored her to a reasonable semblance of her natural self, that wouldn't solve the problem of what to do with her. During their long flight through the mountains and across the desert she'd refused to discuss the hour she'd spent in his cell in San Rosario. It was almost as if it had happened to two other people. More, during their flight, she'd

71

been propriety itself. All he really knew about her was that, whatever the motivation behind her brief lapse from her own personal code had been, Catana de Sandoval y Olmedo was a lady.

Royal helped her up onto the raised walk and led the way into the lobby of the hotel. The management had changed since he'd left. The young clerk was new to Royal.

'I'd like four rooms,' Royal said. 'In a row if you have them.'

The clerk smirked at Catana. 'Four rooms?'

'That's right,' Royal said coldly.

Still smirking, the clerk spun the register around and Royal signed it in a deliberately bold hand—'Major John Royal and party.'

The clerk turned to take the keys from the rack, then turned back and looked at the signature again. 'Oh, come off it, mister,' he said. 'Don't try to be fly with me. Major John Royal is dead.'

Royal took the keys from his hand. 'Don't you believe it, son. I'm very much alive. And you have my permission to spread the good news around.'

The clerk swallowed hard. 'Yes, sir.'

Royal looked across the lobby at the dining room. The evening rush was over. Only a few of the tables were still occupied. 'We'll want some supper, too. So don't let the cook get away.'

'No, sir.'

Royal handed the keys to Tyler. 'Take Catana and Don Jesus upstairs while I see if there's a ladies' store open. If there still are any ladies in Dry Prairie.'

'Whatever you say,' Tyler said. 'But watch yourself, Royal. It was bad enough before I left, but considering the new developments, there are quite a few people in town who are not going to be too happy to see you.'

'That sounds reasonable,' Royal said.

He found what he wanted in the Bon Ton, a dress that looked as if it would fit Catana, a pair of ruffled pantaloons, a *camisilla,* some stockings, a pair of *zapatos,* and paid for them with the few dollars Milt Favor had been able to loan him. Back at the hotel, he knocked softly on the door of the room that had been assigned to Catana and when she didn't answer, he turned the knob and walked in.

The girl turned from the washstand, holding an inadequate towel in front of her. Her voice was as expressionless as her face. 'I am sorry,' she said in Spanish. 'I did not hear you knock.'

Royal tried to look away and couldn't. Nothing had changed during the months that had elapsed. Her slight body was small and compact but finely chiseled. Just looking at her excited him.

Before he made a fool of himself, he picked up the dusty vaquero pants and the wool shirt from the bed and replaced them with the garments he'd bought.

'I think you'll be more comfortable in these. Put them on when you finish your bath.'

'Whatever you say, *señor.*'

Royal became impatient with her. 'You might at least call me John.'

Catana smiled her thin smile. 'After all we have been to each other?'

It was the first reference she'd made to their brief intimacy of the cell. 'You could put it that way,' Royal said. 'One of these days or nights, whether you want to or not, we're going to have to talk about it, Catana. But for right now, get dressed. Tyler and Don Jesus are waiting to take you to supper.'

Her eyes clouded as she asked, 'And you?'

'I have some business to take care of, the first of a number of things I have to attend to.' Royal left the room, closing the door behind him, then opened it again. 'One other thing.'

'*Sí, señor?*'

If Royal didn't know better, behind the expressionless mask that she made of her face, he could swear the girl was laughing at him.

He slammed the door, stopped in at Tyler's room to tell him that he would be back as soon as he could, then descended the stairs to the lobby. He knew how to treat *a married* woman. During his three-year sojourn in Mexico, his cantina conquests had been many and varied. But Catana was a new experience to him. He still didn't know any more about her than he had when she'd walked into the Golden

Rooster and asked, 'You are *el médico?*'

The shades of the bank were drawn and the door was locked but there was a light in the alcove where Mr. Kirby had his desk. Royal rattled the knob of the door, then rapped on the glass.

'Go away,' Mr. Kirby called. 'The bank is closed and won't open again until nine o'clock tomorrow morning.'

Royal rapped on the glass again. 'It's John Royal, Mr. Kirby. Major John Royal, if you prefer.'

There was the scrape of a chair being pushed back from a desk and a moment later Mr. Kirby raised the shade in the door and looked out. 'I told you to go away,' he said hotly. 'If you drunks don't stop pestering me after hours, I—' His mouth gaped open. Then he cried, 'By all that's holy—John Royal!' He unlocked and opened the door and gripped Royal's hand. 'We thought you were dead, John.'

Royal closed the door. 'That seems to be a common mistake in Dry Prairie. It's good to see you, Mr. Kirby.'

The banker drew down the shade and locked the door before he led the way to his desk. 'Believe me, it's good to see you. But where in the name of time have you been?'

'In Mexico. In a little town on the west coast called San Rosario.'

'I guess a lot of the boys have headed south.'

'For various reasons.'

The banker offered Royal a chair. 'I might have known the Yankees couldn't kill a Royal.' He sat behind his desk. 'But I hope this is a social call, John. If it isn't, I'm afraid I have bad news for you.'

'What sort of bad news?'

'You don't have any money on deposit, you know.'

'No, I didn't know that. When I left here I had ten thousand in my account.'

The banker pointed out, 'In a joint account with Mrs. Royal. And there it stayed for years, until about four months ago, when Mrs. Royal came in one morning and closed out the account.'

'Cora drew out all of it?'

'Down to the last penny. And there wasn't a thing I could do. It was a joint account. We thought you were dead. Besides, she had your power of attorney.'

'I know. I gave it to her.'

Mr. Kirby drummed his fingers on his desk. 'I'd hoped when Tim Kelly came back with the thirty thousand dollars he got in Abilene for one of the first trail herds to leave here, Cora might reopen the account. But she didn't.'

'Cora got thirty thousand dollars for one herd?'

'That's the talk around the bars.' The banker sighed and shook his head. 'And now Kelly's dead.'

'How dead?'

'Killed in front of the courthouse this morning. In a gunfight.'

'Who killed him?'

'Old man Johnson.'

'Not Orin Johnson?'

'That's the one.'

'What was the fight about?'

'That's a long story, John. But some months back Orin claimed that Kelly included about four hundred of Johnson's longhorns in the herd Tim was shaping up to drive to Abilene. He called Tim on it, before a dozen witnesses. But instead of Kelly going for his gun, Mrs. Royal pulled a little trick she's pulled several times since then. She reached down in her boot top and came up with a little pearl-handled gun and dared Orin to shoot it out with her. We all had a big laugh about it at the time. Naturally, Orin wouldn't draw on a woman. But this morning, this was court day, when Orin called Kelly out in front of the courthouse, after egging them on, Cora just sort of stepped aside and left the play up to Kelly. And he being nowise as fast with a gun as Orin, he was quite surprised to find himself suddenly dead.'

'What did they do to Johnson?'

'Locked him and his two sons in jail at the courthouse. Or maybe I should say guardhouse, the military having taken over the enforcement of the law. Anyway, if the old man and his boys don't get a fairer trial than the one that ordered Orin off his land and sparked the whole thing in the first place, I wouldn't be surprised if all three of the Johnsons hang.'

Royal held up his hand. 'You're coming too fast for me, Mr. Kirby. Who ordered Orin off his land?'

'Colonel Simmons. He's the Union officer in charge of the local garrison and has been ever since we've been "occupied" and practically disenfranchised.'

'That much I know. But what was the charge against Johnson?'

'Inciting to riot. And that's what Orin did. He was guilty as hell on that count.' The banker nodded and said, 'I was at a couple of meetings myself. We were going to form a group of regulators to try to straighten things out. But now, after what's happened to Orin, I don't imagine it will amount to much more than talk.'

Royal felt ill. All of this had been going on while he'd been trying to drown his hurt pride in tequila. He asked Kirby, 'Do you know a man named Tyler?'

Kirby nodded, 'Of course. He's that Yankee who bought out Big Foot Harper. He owns the spread next to yours. He paid two dollars an acre cash for the eighty thousand acres. And while I ain't seen him around for a spell, I hear he's had some trouble with Cora.'

'That's right,' Royal said. 'That's why he looked me up in Mexico. As he pointed out, the ranch does belong to me and not to Cora. And he figured he could get along much better with me than he could with her.'

'That sounds reasonable.' The banker was grim. 'But I don't know if even you can buck that combination, John. This isn't the first time it's happened. I mean charging a local man with something, then finding him guilty in a military court and ordering him off his land. And somehow, Cora always seems to wind up with his holdings. True, except for Tyler, they haven't been giving any of the big landholders any trouble as yet. But between her and the colonel they sure have been whipsawing the hell out of the small fry.' Kirby was hesitant to mention the subject. 'And while I wouldn't want you to take this badly, John, although they have been fairly careful about it, their relationship beyond that of business is well known in Dry Prairie.'

Royal stood up. 'That's one thing I knew before I came in here.'

'You aim to stay and fight this thing?'

'That's why I came back.'

'How are you fixed for money?'

'I haven't any.'

Kirby opened the door of the safe and took out a small sack of gold coins, then laid several sheaves of bills on top of the sack. 'In that case, I want a piece of the action. Two

79

thousand dollars' worth. You can call it a loan or an investment in good government, whichever you're a mind to.'

Royal stuffed the money in his pockets. 'You'll get it back. Now tell me two last things, Mr. Kirby.'

'If I can.'

'How do we Texans stand politically?'

'Bad. They say we're going to be readmitted into the Union, possibly next year. But since the end of the war, all state and federal officeholders have had to swear they didn't take any part in the rebellion. And, as practically every man in Texas old enough to hold a gun was in the Confederate Army, what it amounts to is that a local man can't even run for dogcatcher. We're being governed by scallawags and carpetbaggers. And the military. Your other question, John?'

'How legal is this proposed vote to divide Texas into five separate states?'

'Legal as you can get,' Kirby answered. 'According to a joint resolution of the Congress, a state, with the consent of its citizens, may divide itself into several states and each may seek admission to the Union.'

'And a date has been set for local voting?'

'One week from today.'

'But will such a vote be legal without the consent of all the people of Texas?'

The banker shrugged. 'Some local lawyers say yes, some say no. But this section will go on record as wanting to divide. Backed as she is by Colonel Simmons' bayonets and her own private army to do the jobs too dirty for the soldiers to dare, I imagine Cora Royal will proceed from there. She'll form her own courts, appoint her own judges, elect her own legislature and, legal or not, the whole thing will be such a mess that twelve Philadelphia lawyers won't be able to untangle it in the next hundred years. Meanwhile Cora will go right on making laws and confiscating property and levying taxes. When it's all over she'll be the richest woman in Texas.'

CHAPTER NINE

The milling crowd on the raised wooden walks had increased. As he walked back toward the hotel, a hard-faced shill wearing a high, fawn-colored beaver hat tried to interest Royal in a keno game. He had to step down in the dust to bypass two fistfights. A half dozen girls in various stages of undress leaned out of their windows and openly solicited his business. As he paused in front of the hotel, two Kiowas, wearing fragments of Union uniforms which identified them as army scouts, staggered past him, sodden drunk.

Royal looked after them thoughtfully. What a peacetime garrison needed of Indian scouts was beyond him. But then, nothing in Dry Prairie made sense. Except for Mr. Kirby, he had still to see one familiar face. And these were the men who would be voting to separate Texas into five states, one of them the State of Royal.

The day had been long and hot. Night had done little to dispel the heat. He stood, buffeted by the crowd on the walk, fanning himself with his hat. He felt he was partly to blame for what was happening to Dry Prairie. His money and his land had made it possible. He'd brought Cora here. Then, confronted with her flagrant unfaithfulness, instead of acting the man and doing something about it, he'd remounted his horse and ridden away.

Refusing to face facts had not solved anything. It never did. If he hadn't spent the last three years trying to drown the memory of what he'd seen and playing the same game with cantina girls that he'd caught Cora playing with a Union colonel, none of this would have happened.

Now it was up to him to straighten things out and he had a week in which to do it. It wasn't much time.

On impulse, instead of going into the hotel, he returned his hat to his head and strode down the walk toward the lockup. The news that he was alive and back in town was spreading. He passed a dozen men he knew. Most of them nodded but seemed hesitant to speak. Royal shrugged and walked on. Just how wide a loop could one Texas woman throw?

The bulk of the courthouse was dark but there was a lighted lantern in the dayroom of the guardhouse. Two blue-uniformed soldiers, so young they still had peach fuzz on their cheeks, were astraddle a bench playing Red Dog with a deck of greasy cards. The equally youthful corporal of the guard was reading a dog-eared newspaper. He looked up, incuriously, as Royal hesitated in the doorway of the dayroom.

'What can we do for you, mister?'

'I'd like to talk to some of the men you're holding.'

'Which ones?'

'Orin and Elijah and Saul Johnson.'

The corporal resumed his perusal of the paper. 'Sorry, but they ain't allowed any visitors. To get in to see those fellows you have to get a pass from Colonel Simmons.'

Royal started a hot reply, then thought better of it. The boy was just carrying out his orders.

'I see,' Royal said. 'Then perhaps you'll tell me where I can find Colonel Simmons.'

The two lads playing Red Dog chortled. The corporal looked up from his paper again. 'That I can't rightly say, sir. He might be in his office. I seen a light in there a few minutes ago. Or he might be in the officers' mess.' He winked at the other youths. 'Then, again, he might have ridden out to have supper with a certain young widow he's sweet on.'

'I see,' Royal repeated. 'Do you mind if I look in his office?'

The corporal inclined his head toward a door leading into a hallway. 'It's a free country, mister. Help yourself.'

Royal walked through the guardroom and down the hall until he came to a door bearing the legend COLONEL SIMMONS. The door was partly ajar. He could see a lamp burning in a bracket on the wall. He knocked on the door, then opened it and went in.

There was no one in the office. Royal went in. On the desk was a framed picture of Cora. Royal turned up the lamp and studied it. The artist who'd painted the miniature had done a good job. He'd captured the exact shading of her raven-black hair and the black velvet of her eyes that had been two factors that had attracted him to her when he'd met her. The faint, cynical smile on her lips was familiar. The firm half rounds of her breasts were as he remembered them. The dress, however, was new. The buffalo hunter's daughter with no shoes and only one shift to her name had climbed a long way up the social ladder since he'd picked her out of a one-room shack on the Brazos.

Royal tried to feel some emotion for his wife but failed. Whatever he'd once felt for her was gone. Now she was just a woman he'd known. A woman who'd cost him three years of his life.

He returned the picture to the desk and walked back to the dayroom and laid a ten-dollar gold piece on the desk behind which the corporal was sitting.

'Yours if you do me a favor.'

'What sort of favor?'

'Buy the Johnsons some tobacco and a jug of whiskey if it's permitted. And you can keep the change.'

The corporal put the gold piece in his pocket. 'It's a deal, mister.'

Royal added, 'And when you give them the tobacco, tell them that Major John Royal is alive and back in town and that he isn't going to let them hang if he has to revive the whole Texas Sixth Army.'

The corporal's friendliness disappeared. 'You shouldn't talk like that, sir. That kind of talk can get you into trouble.'

'That's a chance I'll have to take.'

Out in the night again, Royal walked back to the hotel, trying to sort out his thoughts. It was just as well that Simmons hadn't been in his office. Their personal quarrel was three years old. A few more hours wouldn't make much difference. Besides, he wanted to talk to old man Johnson and a few other old-timers in town to find out how many men he could count on to back his play before he made any definite move.

He was tired. He was hot. He was hungry. Judging from the soiled dishes in the hotel dining room, Jim Tyler had already eaten and left on some business of his own but Don Jesus and Catana were still trying to finish their meal. Trying, because, fortunately or unfortunately, the dress he'd chosen for her not only fitted Catana perfectly, it so emphasized her natural feminine charms that despite her close-cropped hair she'd attracted the amorous attention of a half-drunken rider who was attempting to force himself on her while Don Jesus sat there, trying to keep himself from starting a fight.

As Royal watched from the doorway of the dining room, the rider lost patience with the girl and caught her wrist and tried to pull her to her feet.

'Don't be that way, honey,' he said. 'You know you're too young and pretty to play mattress for a fat old greaser. Come on. Let's you and me have a few drinks. Then we'll go upstairs and have a good time.'

Catana tried to free her wrist. 'Please, *señor.* I have no wish to go with you. Please to allow me to finish my *comida.* I have ridden far this day and I am very hungry.'

'Five dollars,' the rider offered. 'Ten, I might even go as high as twenty. I never had me a girl with short hair before.'

Don Jesus got to his feet and the other man

86

pushed him back into his chair, warning him, 'You stay out of this, old man. I'm one of Mrs. Royal's men, her right-hand man, now Kelly is dead. And if I say this girl goes with me, she goes with me. We run Dry Prairie. *Comprende?*'

Royal crossed the room and tapped the man on the shoulder. 'No. Not completely,' he said. 'Perhaps you'd like to explain it to me. I happen to be Major John Royal.'

The rider started to reach for the butt of his gun with his free hand. Then Royal's words penetrated through the alcohol roaring in his head and he released Catana's wrist and backed a few steps from the table.

'Who did you say you were?'

'I said I was Major John Royal.'

The rider continued to back toward the door of the room. 'Yeah. I can see that now. I've seen tintypes of you. Major John Royal, M.D. Army surgeon. One of the heroes of the late Confederacy.'

He leaned against the doorjamb. 'Well, I'll be damned. I knew there was some reason besides getting drunk and giving the girls a whirl made me ride into town tonight. The name is Mason, Hal Mason, Major. Like you probably heard me say, I ride for your wife.' He grinned meaningfully. 'And is she going to be some surprised at what I have to tell her.' He looked from Royal to Catana and his grin widened. 'No offense, Major. But I can see now why you stayed away so long. That's a right pert little piece of baggage you have there.'

When the man had gone, Royal sat at the table and picked up the grease-stained menu. It was immaterial what the rider told Cora. When he rode out to the ranch in the morning he would inform Cora that he intended to file suit for divorce as soon as the proper papers could be prepared.

Don Jesus was apologetic. 'I didn't know what to do.'

Catana laid a small hand on his arm. *'Gracias,* again, *señor.'* She was puzzled. 'But what did the man mean when he said he could see why you had stayed away so long? What mean this,' she had trouble with the unfamiliar words, 'pert little piece of baggage?'

Royal told her. 'He thought you belonged to me. He thought you were my *querida.'*

'Oh,' the girl said. 'Oh.'

Don Jesus got to his feet again. 'If the *señor* and *señora* will excuse me.' He coughed discreetly. 'I think I will go out on the walk and watch the excitement. We were in the mountains so long and on the desert, I have almost forgotten what people look like.'

'You do that,' Royal laughed. 'And while you're out on the town, Don Jesus, pick out a bar you like. When I get things straightened out, I'll buy it for you to replace the cantina in San Rosario. After all you've done for me, it's

88

the least I can do for you.'

The fat Mexican bowed from the waist. *'Mil gracias, señor.'*

After Don Jesus had gone, Royal suddenly realized—Don Jesus had called Catana *señora*. He was puzzled.

He said, 'Don Jesus just called you *señora*. Was that a slip of the tongue? Or does he know something I don't?'

Catana shrugged her shoulders. 'I didn't think it mattered. It was you who called me *señorita* that first evening we met in the Golden Rooster. When you asked me who I was I merely said my name is Catana de Sandoval y Olmedo.'

Royal became jealous. 'Then you have a husband?'

Catana toyed with her coffee cup. 'I had one.'

'Had one?'

'He has been dead for two years.'

Royal protested, 'But you can't be more than seventeen or eighteen now.'

Catana smiled. *'Sí.* I was only fifteen when I was married.' She shuddered. 'He was a very old man. But it was a marriage arranged by my family as is the custom in my country and I had nothing to say about it.'

'I see,' Royal said. 'Then I take it you didn't love him.'

Catana shook her head. 'Whenever he touched me I wanted to scream. But in his way, he was good to me. He provided generously for my family. But when he died, his sons, older than I was, by another marriage long before, inherited all his money and I returned to San Rosario to live with my mother.'

Royal added what she'd just told him to what he already knew. During their trip here, he'd learned that her mother had died while he'd been in prison. Jim Tyler had contacted the girl through Don Jesus and because he'd killed a man in defense of her honor, she'd agreed to go to the prison and inform him of the arrangement that had been made with *Capitán* Dijon. He knew that the original arrangements had called for her and Don Jesus to guide them to the nearest pass through the coastal range, from which point the two Mexicans were to have returned to San Rosario.

But Dijon had double-crossed Tyler and during the resulting chase Royal had been wounded so Catana had refused to leave them and Don Jesus had been afraid to. But he couldn't understand her attitude toward him—first that hour in his cell, then her subsequent coolness to him. Once he'd recovered his senses and some of his strength, Catana had made it a point of never being alone with him during the long trip to the border.

It seemed strange. When he'd walked in on her tonight while she'd been taking a sponge bath, her only covering a skimpy towel, he'd been the one who'd been flustered. He'd had a feeling that she was laughing at him.

The waitress brought the steak he had ordered but Royal suddenly wasn't hungry. What he really wanted was to be alone with Catana, to tell her how much she meant to him, that when it became possible he would be honored if she would marry him.

But this wasn't the time or place. First he had to settle with Cora. And from what he'd learned so far, that probably wouldn't be easy. A lot of blood might be spilled before the business was over.

Catana asked, 'You do not like your steak?'

'It's all right,' Royal said, 'but . . . '

The girl's eyes narrowed as she looked at him. 'But what? Perhaps the reason you cannot eat is because you are still in love with your *esposa*, this woman who has done so many bad things to you?'

Royal put a forkful of steak in his mouth. 'Don't be ridiculous.'

'Then why do you look so sad? You wanted to return to this town. We are here.'

'Yes,' Royal said, 'I know. But I've come back to a mess.' He had a lot of thinking to do. He wanted to be alone to do it. 'Look, Catana,' he added. 'It's been a long day. Why don't you go upstairs and get yourself a good night's rest?' He added what he thought might be an inducement. 'And in the morning I'll buy you something pretty.'

Catana got slowly to her feet. Her voice started low and built up. 'I see. Don Jesus helped you escape from the firing squad and from *Capitán* Dijon and for this you are going to buy him another cantina. I, too, helped you to escape. So now that we are all safe you are also very grateful to me. So grateful you send me up to my bed like a *niña* who has been naughty.'

Royal protested, 'But, Catana—'

Catana interrupted him. 'And in the morning you will buy me something pretty. *Por favor.* Tell me, Major Royal. What is it you will buy for me tomorrow? A nice gringo husband?'

'Don't be silly, Catana,' Royal said. 'You must know how I feel about you.'

The girl was so angry she didn't hear him. With one swift motion of her hand, she tugged the checked cloth from the table, sending the dishes on it to the floor.

Then, slapping Royal as hard as she could, she sobbed, *'Gracias. Mil gracias, señor,'* and turned and ran up the stairs. The slam of her room door was loud and final.

Royal laid a bill on the table to cover the meals and the damage, then walked to the foot of the stairs and looked up. He doubted it would do any good to knock on Catana's door and say that he was sorry for whatever it was he'd said or done to upset her.

It was quite a homecoming for a man who had been away for three years. He walked out the door onto the walk to wait for Tyler. He wondered what the morning would bring. It was going to be a long night.

CHAPTER TEN

The new clothes were Jim Tyler's idea. The Yankee lawyer had argued, 'Not even a Royal can ride back from the dead looking like a seedy saddle tramp and expect to contend with a going operation. If we want the small ranchers to side with us, we're going to have to give them a leader. And while clothes don't make the man, they do impress the eye. So, while I finish drawing your divorce papers and find a process server with guts enough to serve them, you go down to one of the stores and buy yourself a new outfit.'

Now Royal shifted his weight from one foot to the other as old man Johnson paused in what he was saying to aim an accurate stream of tobacco juice at a curious palm roach scurrying across the floor of the cell.

'So whilst me and the boys are mighty pleased you're still alive, Major, and mighty proud of you coming to see us, I think the best thing you can do is climb on your horse and ride out of town. As I see it, if you don't, you'll probably wind up in here with us. No one can buck a setup like this one. And I can't name ten men to side with you.'

'We'll see,' Royal said. 'We'll see.'

Outside the weather had changed during the night. A cold rain had started to fall. The rainfall in Dry Prairie was sparse but when it did rain it rained hard. There would probably be a gully washer before night.

Dry Prairie looked more normal by daylight. There were no flaring flambeaus on the store fronts, no drunks or shills on the raised wooden sidewalks. The whores were gone from the second-floor windows. The tinny pianos in the saloons were silent. The only people on the walks were housewives with market baskets on their arms.

Don Jesus and Jim Tyler were waiting for him at one of the tables in the hotel dining room.

'How did you make out with Johnson?' Tyler asked him.

Royal told him.

Tyler sighed. 'Then we'll have to do it alone. I didn't pay two dollars an acre for eighty thousand acres to see my investment go down the drain. I didn't pry you away from that firing squad in San Rosario just to be chased by the Mexican Army.' Tyler took an official-looking paper from the pocket of his coat. 'I won't bore you with the legal terminology but this is the official notification to Mrs. Cora

94

Royal that suit for divorce, Royal versus Royal, is being filed against her in the district court. There's only one slight hitch.'

'What's that?'

'I can't find anyone in town with nerve enough to serve it.'

'Why can't I give it to her?'

'Because you're a party to the suit.'

Don Jesus was incredulous. 'There is no man in this *ciudad* who is willing to give the paper to the *señora?*'

'So it seems.'

'But why?'

Tyler told him. 'Because she is going to be very unhappy about it.'

Don Jesus tried to be helpful. 'Perhaps if you would entrust it to me, I could give it to the *señora.* That way I could also ride with the major.'

'It's an idea,' Tyler said. 'How about it, John?'

'Would it be legal?' Royal asked.

Tyler drank the cold coffee left in his cup. 'As legal as anything else in this town.'

'Then it's all right with me,' Royal said. 'But remember now, Don Jesus. As soon as you serve the paper, you ride away from the ranch and come straight back here. This is my problem, not yours.'

'*Sí, señor.*'

'So saying,' Royal said, and stood up and put on his hat and slicker, 'I might as well get it done.'

Tyler followed him out into the rain. 'I don't know if we're playing this smart or not. She's supposed to have fifty riders out there, all drawing more money per month than the marshal of Abilene. And they're not going to look kindly on your taking over the ranch.'

'What do you want me to do? Ask Colonel Simmons for an escort of troops?'

'No. But maybe I'd better round up what boys I have left and go with you.'

Royal wiped rain from his face. 'Thanks. But Cora is my wife and my problem. If I'd done this three years ago, we wouldn't be in this mess.'

'Well, watch yourself.'

Royal eased his gun in its holster. 'Don't worry about me. In spite of the way Johnson talked there must be a few people in town who don't like the way things are being run. And I doubt if either Cora or Colonel Simmons wants any open break until this division business has been voted on and settled one way or another.'

'I'll keep my fingers crossed,' Tyler said. 'But if you aren't back by night, I'm riding out to find out why.'

'Still thinking of your ranch?'

Tyler grinned crookedly. 'Not entirely. Having helped lick you stiff-necked rebels into a reasonable facsimile of submission, I feel it my duty as a former private in the Union Army to guide you back into the paths of virtue and rectitude without allowing you to become a corpus delicti in the process.'

'Thanks for the concern,' Royal said.

He strode down the walk with Don Jesus and they got their horses from the livery stable.

As their horses clattered across the loose planking of the bridge, Don Jesus asked, 'We ride far, *señor?*'

'About twelve miles,' Royal told him.

He still had a lot of thinking to do. The farther he rode from town the more familiar the country became. It was good to be home. He wished he was making the ride under other, more normal conditions. There wasn't a foot of the rolling savanna he didn't know intimately. Every rise, every clump of trees, held a pleasant memory of his boyhood. He'd never seen the wild grass so lush, nor so many fat cattle. It was obvious that during the war, while their owners had been busily engaged in killing each other off, the creatures of the range had continued to breed. Proving something. Possibly that animals, especially Texas longhorns, were smarter than people.

Barely two miles out of town, his meditation was interrupted by the rhythmic thud of racing hoofs behind them. Don Jesus turned in his saddle and shielded his eyes from the rain. *'Dos caballeros,'* he reported. 'Riding fast. They look like *soldados* to me.'

Royal reined his horse off the road and behind a clump of prickly pear and sat waiting in the rain with his slicker pulled back and his right thumb hooked in his gunbelt. He doubted that Cora and her colonel would resort to outright murder to cover their illicit relationship but there was that possibility. When he'd entered the dayroom of the guardhouse that morning to ask Colonel Simmons' adjutant for a pass to see the Johnsons, Simmons had seen to it that the day detail were Regular Army men, veterans of a dozen campaigns and battles. It could have been a lefthanded warning to him that Simmons had might if not right on his side.

The horsemen were plainly visible now. They were two of the soldiers he had seen in the dayroom. The men looked neither to right nor left as they galloped past the clump of brush and disappeared behind the wall of rain between him and the ranch.

Royal urged his horse back onto the road. 'Well, at least,' he said drily, 'we won't arrive unannounced.'

CHAPTER ELEVEN

The steady fall of the rain on the roof of the open gallery was a pleasant sound. After the heat of the last few months, it felt good to be

98

cool. The falling rain increased the fragrance of the blossoms of the late-blooming ratama tree in the courtyard. Cora sat in the big willow rocker that had belonged to John Royal's mother and rocked. All was peaceful and orderly here. She enjoyed her hard-won power. She had no intention of giving up any of it. Cora was concerned but not worried. She believed that when the time came, she could handle John Royal. Her immediate problem was Bill Simmons.

Simmons poured himself another drink and downed it. 'Now let's get this straight, Cora. You've known that your husband was alive for three, nearly four months. And you didn't even bother to tell me.'

The black-haired girl made a gesture of distaste. 'Your getting drunk won't help things any.'

'It does a little,' Simmons said. 'Being a woman, I doubt if you can understand. But it's one thing to make love to—'

Cora finished the sentence for him '. . . a young and willing widow. But something else to go to bed with another man's wife.'

'You could put it that way. Why didn't you tell me that Manuel had told you he'd seen Royal?'

Cora continued to rock. 'There was no need for both of us to worry. Anyway, I didn't have the least idea that John would be fool enough to come back here.' She added bitterly, 'It's all that Jim Tyler's doing. He was afraid I'd take over his spread and knew that John would be a better neighbor than I've been. All you Yankees think of is money.'

'Your motives are purely unselfish, I suppose?'

'No. Exactly the opposite, I'm not ashamed to admit. Have you ever lived in a one-room shack, wondering where your next meal of grits and side meat was coming from?'

'No.'

'Well, I have. With one dress and one shift to my name and no shoes. That's what John Royal took me out of. Because I was young and pretty. Because he wanted the same thing from me that you and all other men want. And I'm not going back to that again. I like being a lady. And I'm going to keep right on being one, no matter what it costs.'

'I can understand that,' Simmons said. 'But what do I do now? Do I put my tail between my legs and crawl? Or do I let Royal call me out and shoot me like you let Johnson shoot Kelly yesterday?'

'I can't see that I'm to blame if Tim was slower with a gun than a sixty-year-old man. Before he took the trail herd to Abilene he begged me to let him handle Johnson.'

Simmons refused to be diverted. 'Well, which is it? What do I do?'

She continued to rock. 'You don't do anything. I'll take care of John Royal.'

'How?'

'I'll think of some way.'

Simmons poured more whiskey into his glass. 'While the boy hero of Shiloh hides behind your skirts or under them?'

'That's not a nice thing for a gentleman to say to a lady,' Cora retorted. 'You know that you shouldn't have stayed here last night. And you know that you shouldn't be drinking this morning. We're too close to putting this thing over to have anything go wrong now.'

Simmons studied his glass. 'I wonder. The only people who are really on our side, who want this division, are the office seekers and saloon men and the gamblers and the pimps and a handful of merchants who are afraid to stand up to you. All the others despise us.'

Cora was complacent about it. 'After next Tuesday it won't make any difference. After next Tuesday they'll take orders from me.'

Simmons walked to the edge of the gallery and stood looking out into the rain. 'They may take them but they won't be happy about it. And just how do you think General Sheridan is going to react when I send a courier to inform him that this section of his Texas-Louisiana District has voted to separate from the rest of Texas?'

'He won't like it,' Cora admitted. 'He may even send more troops to garrison the area. And that will be just fine, as long as you're still in command. We can use the men until we get

101

things stabilized.'

'And after that?'

'You'll resign your commission and we'll get married.'

'Do you think you can manage two husbands?'

Simmons returned to the worn leather couch and stretched out with his drink beside him. 'I don't know, Cora. There are times when I think this whole idea is mad. Even if the vote next Tuesday does go in our favor, the United States Congress isn't going to ratify any separation without the vote of all the people in the state.'

Cora continued to rock. 'We'll cross that bridge when we reach it. If I can run this section of the state the way I want to for just six months, neither of us will ever have to worry about money again.'

'You have something there,' Simmons agreed. 'But don't ask me to arrest Royal and lock him up on some trumped-up charge. I won't. Besides, we still have Tyler to deal with. And he's not only a good Union man, he knows more people in high places than I do.'

Cora stopped rocking. 'Tyler worries me more than John does. I should have had Kelly take care of him the first time he protested that we were illegally branding his spring crop.' She became silent as two horsemen rode into the courtyard. Then she said, 'Two of your men just rode in.'

Simmons got to his feet and took his uniform coat from the back of a chair. He put it on and hurriedly buttoned it as he walked to the edge of the gallery and watched the two soldiers dismount.

'Now what, Sergeant?'

The trooper gave him a stiff salute. 'I thought you ought to know, Colonel. Captain Ames gave Major Royal permission to see the Johnsons this morning.'

Simmons returned the salute. 'Stand easy, Sergeant. And you rode all the way out here to tell me that?'

'No, sir. But after Mr. Royal left the guardhouse, we sort of kept our eyes on him, like you said we should. And after he stopped at the hotel and talked to that fellow Tyler, he saddled up and headed out this way. I thought you might want to know, so we rode on ahead to tell you.'

'Thank you, Sergeant. Is Royal alone?'

'No, sir. He has a Mexican with him. The same Mexican who rode into town with him last night.'

Cora rose from the rocker and joined Simmons at the edge of the gallery. 'Major Royal is riding here?'

'Anyway, in this direction, ma'am.'

'Is he armed?'

'Yes, ma'am. Both him and the Mexican fellow.'

Colonel Simmons nodded curtly. 'That will

be all, Sergeant. You may go. But, with Mrs. Royal's permission, you'd better stop in at the bunkhouse and dry out a bit and have something to eat and drink before you ride back.'

'Thank you, sir.'

The sergeant and his fellow trooper led their horses across the courtyard toward the hitchrack in front of the bunk-house.

Simmons sat down on the edge of the couch. 'I don't get it,' he said. 'The man has been in town since early yesterday evening. A dozen people must have explained the situation to him. He's out of his mind to ride out here.'

Cora smiled thinly. 'Daniel into the lions' den.' She walked into the house and returned wearing riding boots and a slicker over her riding costume. 'Now, if you will excuse me for a few minutes, I want to talk to Hal Mason again. I want to know more about that Mexican girl who's traveling with John.'

Simmons studied her face for a long time without speaking. Then he asked, 'What sort of web are you weaving now, Cora?'

She kissed him lightly on the cheek. 'You'll know when the time comes.'

Simmons gulped down his drink and poured another. 'It's your affair. You're running the show. But you mentioned Daniel a few minutes ago. And if I recall my Bible correctly, when he tangled with the lions, he came out on top.'

'That's true. But I wasn't one of the lions.'

Cora walked through the rain, falling heavily now, to the bunkhouse not far away. Her latest recruit was standing in the open doorway. Cora didn't like the way the man who claimed his name was Captain Marcel Dijon was looking at her. The more she saw of the man the more she regretted the impulse that had led her to add his name to her payroll. He was too handsome, too cynical, too sure of himself. Whenever she was near him she could feel his eyes on her. He was the first man she'd ever met who made her uncertain of her ability to handle any man. There were only two things in his favor. He looked like he would be a fast man with a gun. He, too, wanted John Royal dead.

Dijon stepped aside to allow her to enter the bunkhouse. 'May I ask what brings madame out in the rain?'

Cora shook the rain from her slicker. 'I want to talk to Hal Mason. You may be interested to know that those two soldiers who just rode in brought word that a friend of yours is on his way here.'

'Major Royal?'

'He should ride through the gate any minute.'

Dijon rested his hand on the butt of his gun. '*Merci.*'

'*No,*' Cora said. 'It isn't quite that simple. I

105

don't want him killed here on the ranch. Not unless he provokes a fight.'

'May I ask madame why?'

Cora answered bitterly. 'Because he is a Royal. Because his name means something in this part of Texas. As a doctor, he's treated half the people in the county. He was a major in the Confederate Army and I don't want anyone in Dry Prairie to be able to say I had him murdered.'

Dijon smirked in an amused way. 'You mean until after next Tuesday.'

'That's right.'

'But what if he makes trouble today?'

'Then we'll do whatever has to be done.'

Dijon clicked his heels and bowed from the waist. 'Madame makes her meaning perfectly clear. Now I will tell Mason you wish to see him.'

Cora walked on into the bunkhouse. Some of the men were sleeping. Others were playing cards. A few were drinking coffee with the two Union soldiers. Hiring these men had been expensive but smart. They were so many black aces in the hole. She'd never seen a more motley collection of hired guns. There was nothing they wouldn't do to keep their jobs. If Royal wanted trouble, she was ready for him. But, until after the proposed separation had been voted on, she wanted to avoid violence if she could. If the matter was handled in a clever manner, in spite of what Bill Simmons said, there was a fifty-fifty chance that Congress would ratify the separation. Congressmen weren't any smarter than other men.

Mason was sitting in on one of the card games. He handed his cards to Dijon and joined her. 'You want to see me, Mrs. Royal?'

Cora came directly to the point. 'When you returned to the ranch last night you told Colonel Simmons and myself that you'd met the girl who rode into Dry Prairie with the major.'

'That's right,' Mason said.

'What kind of a girl is she?'

'A little lady, I'd say. Either that or she's plenty stuck on the major. She put up plenty of fuss when I tried to waltz her out of the hotel room for a few drinks and a frolic.'

'And you say she is pretty?'

'Very pretty.'

'How old is she?'

'Seventeen or eighteen.'

That much checked with what Dijon had told her. Cora asked, 'Did you learn her name?'

'No,' Mason admitted. 'I didn't.'

Dijon tossed the cards Mason had handed him into the discard and joined them. 'I can tell you that, madame. Her name is *Señora* Catana de Sandoval y Olmedo.'

'*Señora?*' Cora asked with interest.

'*Oui,* madame. Young widow or wife, I don't

know. But she dyed her blond hair black to disguise herself and spent an hour alone with Major Royal in his cell on the afternoon before he was to face the firing squad.'

'I've heard of the custom,' Cora said drily. She turned back to Mason. 'Are they checked into the hotel together?'

'No,' Mason said. 'They have separate rooms. I made it a point to ask the hotel clerk and he told me that Major Royal insisted on having four rooms.'

'But their rooms are adjoining?'

'Yes, ma'am.'

'Good.'

Mason enthused, 'What I mean, Mrs. Royal, she is really something.'

Mason started to draw an outline of Catana's figure with his hands and Cora stopped him. 'That won't be necessary, Mr. Mason. I'm not at all interested in the physical proportions of Major Royal's inamorata. But you can tell me this. You said she seems to be very fond of Major Royal. How does he feel about her?'

Mason grinned. 'I'd say the feeling is mutual. You should have seen his face when he caught me fooling around with her. For a minute I thought he was going to blow my head off.'

'Good,' Cora repeated. She turned to leave the bunk-house, then turned back. 'You'd better alert the men. There may be trouble.

But tell them I don't want any shooting unless the major starts it.'

'Whatever you say, Mrs. Royal.'

Cora added to Dijon, 'And that includes you, Captain Dijon. My husband may have cost you your commission in the Mexican Army but this is not Mexico. This is South Texas and I give the orders here.'

The former legionnaire drew himself to rigid attention and clicked his heels. 'But of course, madame. And, as I assured you yesterday, I know how to take orders.'

Cora walked back through the rain to the house. Bill Simmons had pulled on his boots and buttoned his tunic again and was buckling on the gunbelt that supported the heavy service revolver.

'I don't think that will be necessary,' Cora said. 'I think I may just have something, Bill. Something that will effectively tie John's hands no matter how badly he may want to make trouble for us.'

Simmons slipped his revolver from its holster and spun the cylinder to be sure the chambers were full. 'Just what has your satanic little mind conjured up now?'

Cora told him. 'Another lion for Daniel. This one has very sharp teeth.'

'Now I know one of us is drunk.'

'You are a legally constituted judge, aren't you?'

'Of this particular district, yes. I'm judge,

jury and prosecutor.'

'Then you could hold a divorce hearing and grant a divorce?'

'As legally as I've done a lot of other things since you got your claws into me.'

Cora dropped her wet slicker on a chair and held up her face to be kissed. 'Good. Then I want to file for a divorce from John Royal, naming one Catana de Sandoval y Olmedo as the other woman.'

Simmons kissed her. 'You're crazy, Cora. Three months ago, at your insistence, I declared Royal legally dead and invested his property in your name. You can't divorce a dead man.'

'No,' Cora agreed. 'But I can make him walk very quietly. You don't know John Royal. I do. He's a very normal, lusty man. He damn near loved me to death the first year we were married. But he is also a gentleman. He'll do anything he can to protect a woman's good name. And if I threaten to drag this little Mexican tart he's living with through a lurid divorce suit, he'll be just that much easier to handle. Besides, it will give the psalm-singing old biddies in Dry Prairie someone to talk about and take their minds off us.'

Simmons released her and picked up the whiskey bottle and his glass. 'You're a she-devil, Cora. I was a fool to ever listen to you.'

Cora walked to the edge of the gallery and peered out through the rain. 'I'd go easy on the whiskey if I were you, Bill. He's a little older and a little late and he's very wet but I believe the major has come home.'

CHAPTER TWELVE

Royal reined in his horse at the gateway in the wall that Cora had built since the night he'd come home from the war some three years before, and sat in the rain looking at the wall and other additions she'd made. The woman had to be a little mad. With the big gate closed, the old home place in which he'd been born was more a fort than a ranch-house.

Don Jesus wiped rain from his eyes. 'If there were but walks on the walls for the sentries it would look like pictures I have seen of the Alamo. But why did you build your *casa* this way, *señor?*'

'I didn't,' Royal said.

He looked toward the gallery. He and Don Jesus were expected. Cora was waiting for him, standing beside a tall, formally attired Union officer. He was probably Colonel William Simmons. Royal paid the man his due. At least Simmons wasn't a coward.

Don Jesus strained to see through the rain. 'The tall, dark-haired woman is your *señora?*'

'That's right.'

'Shall I give her the paper now?'

Royal urged his horse into the courtyard. 'I'll tell you when.'

The new bunkhouse was not far from the gate. As Royal rode past it, two dozen or more men came out of the open door to watch him. All of their faces were unfamiliar to Royal. They all looked like hard characters. They must be part of the private army he'd been told Cora had hired.

He looked back at Cora and was pleased to find that seeing her in the flesh evoked no emotion in him. Not that she wasn't still beautiful. She was more beautiful now at twenty-seven than she'd been at seventeen.

He dismounted in front of the gallery and handed the reins of his horse to Don Jesus. 'Hello, Cora,' he greeted her.

The black-haired woman gave him a thin smile. 'Why, John. How nice to see you. We all thought you were dead. Up until last night, that is. Then one of my riders told me you'd checked into the hotel in Dry Prairie with some little Mexican tart.'

Royal refused to be baited. Cora hadn't changed. Her beauty was all on the surface. Her greeting didn't surprise him. He'd reasoned she'd strike first on the theory that the best defense was to attack. But he had not expected her to involve Catana. He forced himself to smile. 'Part of what you say is true. I did ride into town last night.'

'After seven long years.'

Royal corrected her. 'Three years and some months.'

Cora ignored the correction. 'Well, don't just stand there. Come in out of the rain.'

'Thank you.'

Cora indicated the Union officer. 'I don't believe you and Colonel Simmons have met.'

'No,' Royal said, 'we haven't.'

'Colonel Simmons, Major Royal, late of the Texas Sixth Army. Major Royal, Colonel Simmons, in command of the local Union garrison.'

Simmons stiffly inclined his head. 'Major,' he acknowledged the introduction.

'I'm honored,' Royal said wryly. 'I imagine it's not very often that an old soldier returns from the wars to find his wife being protected by a full colonel of the enemy.'

'I imagine it is very rare,' Simmons agreed.

Sensing motion behind him, Royal glanced over his shoulder and saw that Cora's private army of hired guns had followed Don Jesus and him to the house. They were evidently anticipating a fight between himself and Simmons. The thought amused him. At one time nothing would have kept him from trying to kill the Union officer. Now he just felt sorry for the man.

Cora broke the awkward silence that followed. 'Why don't we all have a drink? After all, the three of us are—'

'I think I know what you're going to say,'

113

Royal interrupted her. 'After all, the three of us are adult, mature people. So why don't we act mature about this? Isn't that what you were going to say, Cora?'

'Something like that,' she said.

Royal nodded. 'That's fine with me. Unless, of course, Colonel Simmons wants to make an issue of it. In that case, I'll be happy to oblige him.'

Simmons was drunk but carrying his whiskey well. He bowed as stiffly as he'd inclined his head. 'At your service, Major. Any time.'

Cora became impatient. 'Oh, for heaven's sake. You make me feel like a dance-hall jade. Let's all stop talking like play actors in a melodrama.' She sat down in the rocking chair and eyed Royal thoughtfully. 'Just what do you want here, John?'

Royal told her. 'My ranch.'

Cora rocked slowly and said, 'Just like that.'

'Like that.'

She continued to rock. 'In other words, after having been gone for years, years in which all of us assumed you were dead, you've ridden back out of nowhere and expect to take over.'

'I do.'

Cora smiled. 'I'm afraid there's one small flaw in your reasoning, John.'

'What's that?' he asked her.

'The ranch no longer belongs to you. It's mine.'

114

'On what do you base that premise?'

'On the premise that when a man dies his property goes to his widow. And, after waiting for you to return for seven years, about three months ago I filed a petition with the local court to have you declared legally dead. My petition was granted.'

Royal looked at Simmons. 'Is that correct, Colonel?'

'Yes. Yes, it is.'

'You signed the papers?'

'Upon what seemed like reasonable evidence. No one in Dry Prairie had seen you for seven years. And a seven-year absence constitutes a presumption of death.'

'I see,' Royal said. 'Well, it seems that I'll have to contest your ruling.'

Cora was amused. 'I wish you luck.'

Royal said, 'I may need it. But as the first step in my resurrection, as one small proof that I am alive—' He motioned to Don Jesus. 'You can serve that paper now.'

The fat Mexican handed the reins of the horses to the man standing nearest him. *'Por favor.'* Then he took the paper Tyler had given him from the crown of his sombrero and presented it to Cora. 'With the *señora's* permission.'

Cora continued to rock as she unfolded it and read the heading aloud. 'Royal versus Royal. How amusing.'

'What's so amusing about me filing a

divorce suit?' Royal asked.

Cora told him. 'A number of things. In the first place, you're legally dead. In the second place, last night I learned that, shall we say, the report of your death had been slightly exaggerated and you were not only alive but you were being unfaithful to me. In fact, you'd been unfaithful to me for some time with a Mexican girl of loose morals who uses the name of *Señora* Catana de Sandoval y Olmedo, so I decided to file suit for divorce also. I filed this morning.'

It was a development Royal had anticipated. He said, 'Suppose we leave Catana out of this.'

Cora shook her head. 'Oh, no. No man walks out on me and stays gone for seven years, then rides back and sues me for being human, especially when he is equally guilty of the same alleged misconduct. Believe me, John, if you force me to, I'll make the name of your little Mexican friend a byword from here to Mexico City. I'll go into court and tell all of Texas what a little tart she is and prove it.'

Royal started a hot retort but his common sense stopped him. Cora was baiting him. She wanted him to lose his head. 'It won't work Cora,' he said quietly. 'You can't wash your own skirts that way. But I didn't ride out here to split straws.'

'Then why did you come?'

'To ask you to get off my ranch.'

'And if I don't?'

'I'll have to use force to recover what is legally mine.'

The black-haired woman laughed. 'Don't be silly. You must have looked around you when you rode in. I'm in the saddle and you know it.' She tore the paper that Tyler had prepared in half and then in fours and dropped the pieces on the floor of the gallery. 'Now take your greasy process server and get off my land before I lose my temper.'

'It won't work, Cora,' Royal repeated in the same calm manner. 'I saw your men when I rode in.'

'And you're not afraid?'

'Not particularly.'

'Then you're a fool.'

'That may be,' Royal admitted. 'But I feel it's only fair to warn you that this is just the beginning. And now I'm speaking of the much larger issue at stake. There is not going to be any division or any separation from the rest of Texas. The only ones who want it are the riffraff you've brought in. All the decent element needs is a leader.'

'And you're that leader?'

'I think there are a few men who will ride with me. In fact, Jim Tyler felt so certain of it that he was willing to spend a great deal of time and money to locate me, then risk his own life to get me back here.'

Cora stood up. 'I think you'd better go now.'

Royal shaped his hat to his head. He'd done

what he'd come to do. He'd gone on record. He nodded to Don Jesus. 'All right. Let's ride.'

'*Sí, señor.*'

Don Jesus started to take the reins of his horse from the man holding them.

'*Gracias, señor,*' he began, then realized that the man looking back at him through the rain was Dijon. What followed was reflex action. The former cantina owner had spent too many long days and nights in the mountains and in the desert being hunted by Dijon to think coherently. He instinctively reached for his gun and the other man's first bullet spun him around and left him clinging to one of the uprights of the gallery for support.

As instinctively, Royal drew his gun and, furious, Cora stepped out into the rain between the two men. 'I told you I didn't want any shooting on the ranch.'

Dijon holstered his gun. 'May I remind you, madame, that I wasn't the first to draw.'

'Even so,' Cora said.

Royal holstered his gun and helped Don Jesus to a sitting position and used his pocket knife to cut away the wounded man's shirt. Dijon's bullet had struck the Mexican high on the chest but it was impossible to tell by a cursory examination whether it had gone through his lung. All he could tell was that the wound was bleeding profusely.

He straightened and looked at Cora but before he could speak, she said curtly, 'Now get him out of here before there is any more trouble.'

Royal protested, 'But the man is in no condition to ride.'

'Even so. I didn't ask you to come here. I am asking you to leave.'

'Then let me use the buckboard to get him back to town.'

Cora considered the request and rejected it. 'No. I don't owe either of you anything. My man didn't start this. Yours did. You rode out here. You can ride back.'

There was a clean linen serviette lying beside the bottle of whiskey on the table. Royal poured whiskey on the wound in a crude attempt to forestall infection, then used the napkin to staunch the flow of blood as best he could and tied the crude bandage in place with a towel that Manuel brought him.

'It is best you go now, Major,' the major-domo said sadly. '*Mucho* bad times have come to the *rancho.*'

Royal helped Don Jesus to his feet and through the rain to his horse. It wasn't a question of the man being able to ride. He had to ride. If he could get him back to Dry Prairie there would be a chance of saving his life.

With Royal's help, Don Jesus managed to climb into his saddle and Royal mounted his own horse and supported the other man with one arm.

'I won't forget this, Cora.'

The girl was back on the gallery, unpinning her rain-sodden, long black hair preparatory to having it dried with the towel Conchita was holding. 'Nor I,' she said coldly, and turned away.

Royal sat a moment longer looking from Cora to the wet faces of the men clustered around him. Even Dijon looked smug. Royal had made the first play and lost. Once the news of the incident reached Dry Prairie Cora would be more firmly entrenched than ever. Nothing succeeded like success. People always liked to string along with a winner.

He turned the heads of the horses and rode out of the courtyard, supporting Don Jesus. They had twelve miles to go and from the way Don Jesus was wheezing and rolling in his saddle, he doubted that he would make the first mile.

He'd ridden less than a quarter of a mile when a buckboard, drawn by a team of matched bays, careened from behind them and stopped.

His face completely devoid of expression, Colonel Simmons said, 'It's a long ride for a wounded man, Major. You'd better put your friend in my buckboard.'

With Simmons' help, Royal transferred Don Jesus from his horse to the bed of the wagon and shielded him from the rain with a piece of tarpaulin stamped U.S.A. in big block letters.

The Union officer made his position clear.

'There are some things a man can do and some he can't. But this does not change anything between us. I'm still at your service any time you may care to call me.'

'I understand,' Royal said.

CHAPTER THIRTEEN

It was late afternoon on the third day after Dijon had shot Don Jesus. Deep purple shadows had begun to reach out of the great pear thicket behind the small ranch house when Royal rode down the Frio Arroyo and reined in his horse at the crude fence that inclosed the Nels Nielsen home place.

All trace of the recent rain was gone. A blond young woman, holding a baby in her arms, was standing in the doorway watching two towheaded four-year-olds playing in the dust in the yard. When she saw Royal she called to them and the boys ran to her and peered out at Royal from behind her sun-faded skirt.

Royal touched the brim of his hat. 'Mrs. Nielsen?'

The young woman merely looked back at him without returning his greeting. Close by, penned in a brush corral, a wobbly-legged calf was bleating plaintively as Nielsen tried to fend it away so he could milk its outraged mother.

Royal dismounted and held the calf away from the cow so the rancher could milk it with both hands.

'Thanks, Major,' Nielsen said cordially. 'As you can see, we've got us a new youngun. And since all this started, the missus—' Nielsen shrugged. 'Well, you know how women are. They get to thinking on things and worrying and they dry up faster than a spooked range critter.'

'Yes,' Royal said, 'I know.'

The woman called from the doorway of the house. 'Don't you take no sides now, Nels. You mind what you promised. Remember, we've got three younguns to think of.'

Royal continued to struggle with the determined calf. 'Judging from what Mrs. Nielsen just said, Jim Tyler must have been here.'

The rancher shook his head. 'No. But Max Carter came by late yesterday afternoon and he said that you and Tyler had talked to his wife and that you were riding around talking to some of the boys.'

'That's right. For the last three days.'

'How you making out?'

'We aren't,' Royal admitted. 'All the men we've talked to so far are afraid to climb down off the fence.'

'That figures,' Nielsen said. Content with what he had in his pail, he stood up and laid his one-legged stool on top of the brush corral. 'And I'm afraid you're not going to make out any better here.'

Royal protested, 'But somebody has to take a stand, Nels.'

The rancher agreed with him, and in a grim manner he added, 'Sure. That's what old Orin Johnson preached. And look where it got him and his two boys. They'll be lucky if they don't hang. And like the missus just said, I've got three younguns to think of.'

Royal released the calf. 'All right, Nels. Tell me this. How much of your spread do you think will be left for your boys if what Mrs. Royal is planning goes through?'

The rancher shrugged. 'That's hard to say. But when a man gets pushed into a corner he doesn't stop to think of what's going to happen five or ten years from now. And me and the missus, we talked it over and we figure if we walk real quiet and don't stir up any dust to attract attention to us, maybe Mrs. Royal will leave us be. We don't have much of a spread nohow.'

Royal rested his hip against the fence. 'You don't have a chance of getting off without being hurt in some way, Nielsen. No one in this section of Texas has. Not even the large landholders. If Mrs. Royal manages to swing this division, if the proposal to separate gets enough votes next Tuesday, once we're cut off from the rest of Texas, she'll burn her brand on everything she sees.'

Nielsen bit a chew from his plug of tobacco. 'That can be. But you tried to stop her, didn't you? And the way I heard it, she was so afeared of you she ordered you off your own ranch and that's why you're bunking with Tyler.'

Royal was also grim as he said, 'News does get around. Especially if it's bad. Then we can't count on you, Nels?'

The rancher said, 'Let's put it this way, Major. I'd druther wait and see which way the wind blows.'

'But by then it may be too late.'

Nielsen agreed with him. 'Could be. But the way I see it, John, you came home three years too late. Right now, all I'm figuring on is holding on till spring. Then I aim to trail a herd to Abilene and get me some of that fourteen dollars a critter money.'

'If you have any cattle left by then.'

'That's a chance I'll have to take.'

'Besides, by then you may not even be living in Texas.'

Nielsen spat tobacco juice into the dust. 'That's a tough one to chew on. Believe me, John. I don't hold any more with this division business than I do with the thieving and the killing that's been going on.'

'Then why not throw in with us? If we band together we can fight it.'

The rancher shook his head. 'I'm sorry. But

you heard what the missus said. I promised her.' He made certain that his wife was still in the doorway and couldn't hear him. 'But I tell you what, Major. You show me that we have a chance to beat Mrs. Royal's hired guns and the Union garrison in Dry Prairie and I'm your huckleberry.'

'You mean you'll side with me and Jim Tyler?'

Nielsen made his position clear. 'I mean I'll side with law and order and keeping Texas whole. But only if you can show me we have a chance to win.'

Mrs. Nielsen left the doorway and waded the dust in the yard to the fence. 'You mind what I say, Nels. It's better to be safe than proud. We don't want none of Mrs. Royal's riders burning us out or running off our cattle.' She sniffed as she looked at Royal. 'Anyway, I can't see that one side is any better than the other. To my mind, it's a case of the pot calling the kettle black.'

Royal mounted his horse. 'Well, thanks for that much at least, Nels. Will I see you in town Tuesday?'

The rancher shrugged. 'I rode in this morning and I'll probably be there Tuesday. But don't look for me to vote one way or the other. My common sense won't let me vote yes and I'm too hemmed in to vote no.'

Royal touched the brim of his hat to Mrs. Nielsen and rode back up the arroyo.

Practically every small rancher had reacted the same way Nielsen had. None of them approved of Cora or her plans but they were hesitant to take a stand for fear of calling attention to themselves. Mrs. Nielsens coolness, however, was something new. He wished he knew what she'd meant by saying that to her mind it was a case of the pot calling the kettle black.

The shot came from a thick clump of pear trees several hundred yards away and it tugged his hat from his head. Royal slipped his Winchester from its sheath and flung himself down on the floor of the wash, ready to return the fire. But there was no second shot or anyone or anything at which to shoot.

He lay for a good five minutes, waiting. Then he picked his hat from the ground and stood up and mounted his horse. It was the second time it had happened. He imagined it was Dijon doing the shooting. It was the sort of thing the former legionnaire would do. He'd cost Dijon his commission and only God and Dijon knew how much graft as temporary *comandante* of the prison in San Rosario. This toying with him, showing him how easy it would be to kill him, was the kind of thing that would appeal to the Frenchman's twisted mind.

Night had fallen by the time he reached Jim Tyler's ranch. The still air in the courtyard was heavy with the fragrance of highly spiced food.

Catana was waiting on the gallery.

'Did you have any luck today?' she asked.

Royal sprawled, exhausted, in one of the big rawhide chairs. 'None. I talked to a dozen men, but all of them, for one reason or another, are afraid to stand up and be counted.'

Catana called a vaquero to take care of his horse. 'Perhaps tomorrow will be better.'

Royal allowed her to help him take off his boots. 'I doubt it. How's Don Jesus?'

'Better,' Catana said. 'Much better.' She brought him a small glass of tequila and a slice of lemon and a dipper of cool water. 'Right now he's sleeping but he sat up most of the afternoon talking about what a good *médico* you are.' She put a slight edge on her voice. 'And of the cantina you are going to buy him.'

Royal drank the tequila and sucked the lemon, then drank the water. He liked being with Catana. He liked having her do things for him. He liked doing things for her. But, after all, he was thirty-five to her seventeen or eighteen. Having been disappointed once in marriage, the girl deserved something better than another old man. For all he knew, he might be dead by this time tomorrow night. Dijon, if it was Dijon who was shooting at him, was not a man to give up easily.

Royal carried his boots into the main room of the ranch house. 'Hasn't Tyler come back yet?'

Catana ran her fingers through her short hair. Now that it had grown a little longer and she'd cut off the black ends, she was beginning to look more like the girl he'd first met in the Golden Rooster. 'No. Not yet,' she told him, as she turned up the wick of the lamp. 'But right after you both rode away this morning, a man came out from town and left a *carta* for you.'

'A letter? From whom?' Royal asked.

Catana said, 'He didn't say.'

She took a large manila envelope from Tyler's desk and watched him thoughtfully as he opened it. He slipped the enclosure from the unsealed envelope and read it.

Simmons had meant what he'd said in the rain when he'd offered the use of his buckboard to get Don Jesus into town. The colonel was in too deeply to change sides. The enclosure was an official notification that, in his capacity as the military commander of the district, Colonel William Simmons, sitting as district judge, had granted one Cora Royal a divorce from one John Royal, the plaintiff claiming that on numerous occasions the said John Royal had committed adultery with one *Señora* Catana de Sandoval y Olmedo.

'What does it say?' Catana asked.

Royal put the notice and the envelope in his pocket. 'It isn't important. Nothing could be less important right now.'

The girl looked disappointed but made no comment. Tyler rode in a few minutes later.

His mood was as sour as Royal's. 'And how did you make out?' he asked.

Royal told him, and then asked, 'And you?'

'About the same,' Tyler said. 'Let me wash off some of this dust and I'll tell you about it over supper.'

It was a good meal. Royal should have enjoyed it. He didn't. For some reason Catana was in one of her sullen moods. He felt that he'd let Tyler down. The lawyer had spent a lot of time and money trailing him to San Rosario in the belief that the Royal name would carry more weight than it did.

Toward the end of the meal, Tyler took the latest edition of the four-page Dry Prairie *Clarion,* a weekly, from his pocket and laid it on the table. 'This just came out this morning. I don't imagine you've seen one.'

Royal looked at the headline and winced. There'd been reason for Mrs. Nielsen to act the way she had. Cora wasn't missing a bet. Not content with terrorizing the more reputable male element, she'd turned their God-fearing, moral wives against him. He hoped that Catana didn't read English as well as she spoke it. The headline read:

CORA ROYAL DIVORCES MAJOR; CHARGES ADULTERY

The story was spicy. It alleged the offense had been committed with one *Señora* Catana de Sandoval y Olmedo, a well-known, high-priced Mexican courtesan who made it a practice to console condemned federal prisoners in their cells, that she had so consoled Royal and he had become so enamored of her that after his escape, he had insisted that she accompany him north and that even now, he was living in sin with her.

Catana tapped the headline with one finger. *'No comprende.'*

Royal put the paper aside. 'It's nothing,' he lied. 'Just a local story.'

Tyler handed him a smaller, folded piece of paper. 'Nor do I suppose you've seen one of these. They're not supposed to come out till Tuesday but Mr. Kirby sneaked one out of the print shop.'

Royal unfolded the printed ballot and studied it with interest. Come Tuesday, the voters in the coming election were going to have quite a choice. Along with the main and highly controversial issue, Cora had nominated a full slate of candidates for the proposed new state, ranging from governor and tax assessor down to county offices. Except for one name, all the nominees known to Royal were local scallawags and carpetbaggers who would have a vested interest in the new state.

Royal tapped the name of the nominee for governor. 'I may be grasping at straws, but we may have something here. It looks to me as if Cora has gone a bit too far.'

'You mean in nominating Simmons for governor?'

'That's right.'

'I talked that over with Mr. Kirby,' Tyler said. 'And while Simmons is an alcoholic and venal, he isn't a complete fool. So Kirby and I came to the conclusion it may just be that he hasn't seen a ballot, that he doesn't know that Cora is running him for governor.'

Royal continued the train of thought. 'That's the way her mind would work. And I think I know why she put his name on the ballot instead of her own. She knows that even the saloon men and gamblers and local scallawags would be hesitant to vote for a woman. If this thing does go through, she has to have someone in the big chair whom she can control. She probably has enough on Simmons to have him put away in a federal prison for life.' Royal thought a moment. Then he asked, 'Who is the Union general in command of the Texas-Louisiana Military District?'

'Phil Sheridan.'

'What kind of a soldier is he?'

'A good one. He was a first lieutenant when the war broke out and made brigadier in little less than a year.'

'Do you think he's the kind of man who would stand for a steal like this, who would stand for one of his men stepping as far out of line as Simmons has?'

'I doubt it.'

'Good,' Royal said. He refolded the ballot and handed it to Tyler. 'Have one of your riders, someone you can trust, get this to Sheridan as fast as he can. Tell him he is not to give it to anyone but the general.' Royal became eager. 'Meanwhile we'll create some diversion of our own. If the locals want to be shown that we have a chance of winning before they stick out their necks, we'll show them.'

'How?' Tyler asked.

Royal told him. 'By breaking the three Johnsons out of jail.'

CHAPTER FOURTEEN

Father Alejandro had lighted the candles in the chapel of the mission. The bell in the tower of the frame church the Baptists had built on the bank of Gilmore Creek was tolling the faithful to worship. But the bell and the candles were the only signs that it was a Sunday evening. The crowd on the walks was as thick as any other night. Dry Prairie looked and sounded and smelled the same as it had on the night that Royal had come home.

Tyler rode his horse easily. 'As Don Jesus would say, every night—fiesta. Every freeloader and highbinder in Texas, not to mention a quorum of politicians from Austin, must have crowded in to see how the vote goes on Tuesday. You should be proud. Not every man has the prospect of having a state named after him. Especially a Johnny Reb whose side just lost a war.'

'I'm not impressed,' Royal said drily.

He rode slumped in his saddle, listening to the blare of the music and the drunken laughter wafting through the batwing doors. Every now and then the unseasonable heat of the night was rocked by a series of shots as some drunk emptied his gun at the stars or some other drunk.

Tyler confided, 'It's the single shot that still worries me. I worried about it all through the war. But they tell me you never hear the really important one.'

Royal transferred the reins to his left hand. 'So I've heard.'

At Gilmore Creek, instead of crossing the bridge, the two men turned their horses and rode back the way they had come, making certain it was known they were in town. If they did succeed in breaking the three Johnsons out of the lockup they wanted everyone to know to whom the credit belonged.

He had no way of knowing but Royal thought it would be fairly easy to do what they'd come to do. If normal army procedure was followed, by right of seniority the veterans he'd seen, having their choice of tours of duty, were probably asleep or drunk in one of the saloons along the single main street while the beardless recruits were sweating out the long, dull hours of the night detail. Equally important would be the element of surprise. Colonel Simmons might have been a good soldier while the guns were still shooting but now that he'd been assigned to garrison duty, he had no reason to suspect a frontal attack on his guardhouse.

As they passed the halfway mark, a rider coming from the other way turned in his saddle and looked at them. It was Hal Mason, Cora's new foreman. He gave them a suspicious glance, then rode on.

The business section of the street pinched out once they'd passed the livery stable. From here on there was nothing but a few small adobe dwellings, the blacksmith shop and the courthouse. Catana was waiting where they'd left her, sitting in Tyler's buckboard under the cottonwoods, speaking soothingly to the team from time to time. In the faint moonlight filtering through the leafy branches of the trees she looked very small and fragile but determined.

Royal dismounted and trailed the reins. 'Do you think anyone saw you waiting here?'

The girl shook her head. 'No. A number of *caballeros* rode by but they did not see me. It is too dark here under the trees.'

'And you're certain you can handle the team?'

'*Sí.*'

'Don't worry about her,' Tyler whispered. 'She only has to drive as far as the hotel. You understand now, Catana. You are to wait in the hotel lobby until Major Royal comes for you.'

'I will remember.'

Royal untied the three saddled horses from the right rear wheel of the buckboard and retied them to a sapling. 'We'll cut this thing as planned.' He checked to make sure there were rifles in the three saddle scabbards and a gunbelt on every horn.

'Are we ready to go?' Tyler asked.

'As ready as we'll ever be,' Royal said.

'Then let's dance.' Tyler unhooked the off-trace on the near side of the wagon and used the butt of his gun to crack the metal link he'd previously weakened. Then, dropping the trace to the ground, he nodded to the girl. 'It's time for you to go into your act.'

'*Sí,*' the blond girl slapped the back of the team with the reins. '*Adelante.*'

With the loose end of the whiffle tree alternately banging the nigh horse's hock and buttock and dragging the dust, the team sawed ahead unevenly and Catana barely managed to stop them on the dark side of the yellow pool of light spilling out of the open door of the dayroom.

Tyler and Royal waited until Catana got out of the buckboard. Then they walked through the trees to the courthouse and stood with their backs pressed to the wall, looking sideways through the lighted window.

The young corporal of the guard was using his knife to carve his initials on the scarred desktop. Two other troopers, equally as young and as bored, were straddling the bench playing Red Dog. When Catana appeared in the doorway, they all stopped being bored.

The corporal got to his feet, hastily buttoning his blouse into a semblance of military smartness. 'Yes, miss?' he said, hopefully. 'Is there something I can do for you?'

Catana smiled at him shyly. *'Perdoneme.'* She pretended to have difficulty finding the proper English words. 'Is something the matter with, how you say, *arreos dos caballos.'* She found the English word. 'Ah, yes. Har-ness. Is something the matter with the har-ness of my team.' While the three youthful soldiers watched her, fascinated, she made a see-sawing motion with her arms and shoulders. 'The *caballos* go so.' She turned her smile on full. 'And when I saw the light, I thought, perhaps, you *soldados* would be so kind as to help me.'

The young corporal translated, 'There's something the matter with the harness and her team seesaws and she wants to know if we'll help her.'

The card players got to their feet so fast

they overturned the bench on which they'd been sitting, but the corporal beat them to the door.

'Of course,' he beamed. 'We'll be very happy to help you, Miss—?'

'Gomez. *Señorita* Gomez,' Catana smiled.

She turned and walked back toward the buckboard and the three-man guardhouse detail followed as fascinated by the undulation of her hips as they had been by the seesaw motion of her shoulders.

'Be careful they don't hear us,' Royal whispered.

Tyler was amused. 'Listen to the man. I'd give half of my spread to be that young again. Right now, they wouldn't hear a cannon go off.'

Royal slipped into the guardhouse, followed by Tyler, and walked directly to the peg where on his previous visit he'd seen the guard hang the keys to the cells. The third one he tried fitted the lock of the Johnsons' cell door.

'It's about time you showed up,' Johnson said. 'We'd most give you out.'

'Now, Pa,' one of his sons said.

Royal silenced both of them. 'Keep your voices down. We're doing this the easy way.'

'Who's we?' Johnson asked.

'Jim Tyler and myself.'

'You mean the two of you are cutting this alone?'

'That's right.' Royal gave them their

instructions. 'When we leave here you walk down the hall and out the back door of the courthouse. There are horses and guns waiting for you in the cottonwoods. Once you're mounted, get out of town fast and without being seen if you can. We'll try to give you a few hours' start on any patrol sent out to look for you. But tomorrow morning, we'd appreciate it if you would circle around the back country and do a little talking. War talk.'

Old man Johnson grasped the situation instantly. 'Some of the boys are still straddling the fence, eh?'

'Most of them,' Royal said.

Johnson swore softly. 'I might have figured that when you had to use a Yankee to help pry us out of here. All right. Me and the boys will circulate and we'll talk. And we'll be back here in town Tuesday morning.'

Royal said, 'You'd better not risk that, Mr. Johnson.'

The old man assured him, 'I wouldn't miss being here for a barrel of monkeys. If we kin just get a few of the boys to side with us, it should be the goldangest fandango a man ever saw.'

'Pa's a snoozer, ain't he?' one of his sons said with pride.

'He's a snoozer,' Royal agreed.

He watched the three big men stride down the dark hall and out the back door of the courthouse, then he returned to where Tyler

138

was covering Catana from one of the unlighted windows in the building. 'How is she doing?'

'Fine,' Tyler said in a whisper. 'Between telling her how pretty she is and trying to find out where she lives and if she has a steady boy friend, the boys are patching the trace with a piece of wire.'

Royal glowered out the window. The young soldiers were drawing out what should have been a simple repair job for as long as they possibly could. The waiting seemed to go on forever, with the girl in constant danger that the officer of the day might show up on one of his rounds. He was relieved when he heard her say:

'*Gracias.* You have been much kind, *senors.*'

One of the boys helped her into the buckboard. She clucked to the team. There was a slap of the reins and a creaking of leather as the team leaned into the harness. Then the measured clop of hoofs merged with the distant music.

The three soldiers came in the door of the dayroom comparing notes on Catana. She'd said this to the corporal. She'd said that to another. They were all agreed on two points. She was a good girl. And she was one of the prettiest girls any of them had ever seen.

The corporal suddenly noticed that the door leading to the cell block was ajar. He took a step forward to close it and saw Royal and Tyler.

'I wouldn't,' Tyler warned him as he started to reach for one of the rifles on the rack. 'I wouldn't advise any of you to try anything foolish. The last thing we want is to hurt you.'

The corporal glowered at Royal. 'You're the man who wanted to see the Johnsons.'

'That's right,' Royal said. 'And I saw them. Now if the three of you will kindly walk back toward the cells. As Mr. Tyler has remarked, the last thing we want to do is hurt you.'

'He doesn't want us to be hurt,' one boy said indignantly. 'That's a good one. We'll all serve time for this. Deserted our post, that's what we did. No wonder that Mex girl talked so sweet. She was working with them.'

Tyler motioned to the open cell in which the Johnsons had been a few minutes before. 'Inside and be quick about it.'

The three youths entered the cell with set faces and Tyler continued to cover them with his gun while Royal, working as rapidly as he could, gagged them with their neck cloths, then bound their wrists and ankles with the strips of rawhide the two men had brought with them from the ranch. Then he and Tyler left the cell and locked it, and walked down the hall to the rear door and out.

The three horses they'd brought for the Johnsons were no longer in the clump of cottonwoods. As Royal mounted his own horse, Tyler indicated the ring of keys. 'Throw those away before you pick up Catana. I'll cover things down here to give you time to get out of town. Then I'll meet you on the other side of the bridge.'

Royal felt a mild reaction as he sat his horse. For some reason his fingertips tingled. His breathing was shallow. He tried to look through the dark wall of night around the courthouse.

Tyler asked sharply, 'Well, John? Why don't you move out?'

'I don't like the feeling I have,' Royal said. 'It was too easy.'

'Oh for heaven's sake, Royal. Get hold of yourself. Too easy or not, we did it. Now go get Catana and let's get the devil out of here.'

Royal nodded and rode out of the grove and up the street but his uneasy feeling rode with him. It might just be that Simmons was smarter than they'd thought him to be. Perhaps the man hadn't wanted to hang the Johnsons and for that reason had posted a vulnerable guard. But Simmons' concern didn't extend to him. He was a potentially dangerous enemy. The short hairs on the back of Royal's neck bristled. He'd had all the prison he wanted. He didn't have the least idea what the penalty was for helping a federal prisoner escape. But whatever it was, if and when he and Jim Tyler were caught, they were guilty on three counts.

As he rode past it, he threw the ring of keys up on the flat roof of the blacksmith shop, then roweled his horse into a faster walk and had to stop a block short of his destination as a fight erupted in one of the saloons and boiled over onto the walk and eventually into the street.

Egged on by a shrill-voiced dance-hall girl and the supporters of each man, two drunken riders wrestled their way off the walk into the dust. Then, mouthing curses, both men staggered to their feet, drew their guns and emptied them at each other while the crowd struggled frantically to get out of their line of fire. Both men were so drunk that even at the close range they missed each other, and the only damage done was to the big plate-glass window in the bank and a smaller window in the door of the Bon Ton. Their guns empty, they exchanged a few more hot words, then allowed their friends to lead them away. When the crowd in the street had thinned out sufficiently, Royal rode on and tied his horse to the hitchrack in front of the hotel.

The team and the buckboard were waiting. Royal examined the repaired trace. The young soldiers had done a good job. The trace should hold.

He stepped out on the walk and entered the hotel. Time was of the essence now. The Union O.D. might discover the escape of the Johnsons at any moment. He looked for but couldn't find Catana in the lobby but the clerk who'd been on duty the night he'd first ridden in was standing behind his desk, reading a Police *Gazette.*

Royal strode up. 'Where is she?'

The clerk lowered the magazine and his thin face paled. It seemed an effort for him to speak. 'Oh, no,' he stammered. 'Please. Don't do this to me, Major. Please go away. You're dead.'

Royal gripped him by the front of his coat. 'What the devil are you talking about? I asked you a question. Where is she?'

The clerk recovered some of his composure. 'Then—you aren't dead.'

'What do you mean?' Royal asked him.

'Well,' the clerk gulped, 'right after we heard all those shots, Mr. Mason rushed in and said that you'd had a gunfight with someone named Captain Dijon and that you were dying and wanted to see a Miss Catana de Sandoval y Olmedo before you died. That's why I was so frightened when you first came in.'

'The girl,' Royal said. 'Where is she?'

'Well, I don't rightly know that, Major. When Mr. Mason said what he did she jumped up and said that was her name and she left with him. And the next thing I know you come in here not shot at all and scare the hell out of me.'

CHAPTER FIFTEEN

Royal released the clerk and strode out to the walk. He looked up the street and then down it. There was no sign of either Catana or Mason. He hadn't really expected there would be. By now, escorted by Cora's foreman, Catana was well on her way to the ranch to be held as hostage for Royal's future good behavior.

Cora was smarter than he'd given her credit for being. She'd put her claws in the tenderest spot in the soft belly of the revolt against her. Cora knew he would not sacrifice Catana or any woman, for that matter, to keep Texas from being divided.

If Cora harmed Catana or allowed her to be harmed, he'd kill her. He'd strangle her with his bare hands if it was the last thing he ever did.

In the saloon next door to the hotel a fiddler was scraping his bow across his strings, while a brassy voiced girl sang:

'Mush-a-ring-a-ring-a-rah!
Whack fol'd the dady oh! . . .'

For the first time since he'd left San Rosario, Royal felt that he had to have a drink. He pushed open the batwings and found a place at the bar and ordered whiskey. It tasted good but it wasn't the solution to his problem. He'd tried that route once.

Royal dropped one of the gold pieces that Mr. Kirby had loaned him on the bar. While he stood waiting for his change, one of the girls pushed in beside him and smiled.

'How about it, honey?'

Royal picked up his change. At least the girls in San Rosario had been young and clean. This one looked like she needed a bath. He doubted that she'd combed her hair in a week.

'Thanks, no,' he said drily.

Back on the walk again, he looked up the street toward Gilmore Creek. He'd have to ride up and see but he felt sure Tyler would not be there.

He'd had reason to feel uneasy. Mason had seen them ride into town. Mason had been riding from the direction of the courthouse. Despite Catana's assurance to the contrary, Mason could have seen her and the buckboard in the clump of cottonwoods. Of course the whole thing could have been a trap and Mason could have been expecting them. With so much at stake and with money passing from hand to hand so freely, any of a half dozen people could have sold them out. Tyler's cook. One of his riders. The doe-eyed Mexican girl who had waited on table while they'd made their plans.

Royal untied his horse and rode up to the

bridge. Jim Tyler had either ridden on or he'd never reached this spot. It was something he had to know. He turned his horse's head again and rode down the boisterous street toward the court-house momentarily expecting to be stopped.

He permitted himself to be bitter. Of course. The ease with which they'd been able to free the Johnsons, the drunken brawl blocking the street, the shots that had not hit anyone, they'd all been part of the plot. He and Jim were a hell of a pair of ex-soldiers. They'd been outflanked and outmaneuvered.

The courthouse was lighted now and the hitching rails were lined with saddled horses, all having army saddle blankets, and the letters U.S.A. burned on their sleek haunches. There was a constant coming and going of soldiers in and out of the dayroom. Jim Tyler was standing under guard in the room with Captain Ames and Colonel Simmons questioning him.

Royal turned off the road and went back through the narrow streets and lanes skirting the town toward the creek.

Royal splashed his horse across the shallow creek, then cut across country to the road leading out to his ranch. Technically, he thought grimly, Cora's ranch, now that she'd had him declared legally dead and her Union soldier lover had recorded his property in her name.

From time to time he stopped to listen but could hear no sounds of pursuit. If the soldiers were looking for him, they were confining their search to the main street and environs of Dry Prairie.

The moon had set by the time he reached the draw a quarter of a mile from the ranch. Royal dismounted and tethered his horse to a tree. He made his way through the night until he could see the big gate leading to the ranch. It was open. In the darkness he couldn't tell whether or not a guard had been posted.

While he stood trying to figure some way to slip through the gate unobserved, a deeper shadow of black materialized in the night and moved toward him. Royal drew his gun.

'*Quién es?*'

Royal stood still, not answering and with his gun ready. Then the figure spoke and Royal sighed, relieved, and put away his gun when he recognized the voice.

'It is Manuel, *señor,*' the aged man whispered. 'I have been waiting these long hours for you. But you should not have come here. It is what the *señora* wants.'

Royal nodded. He'd figured that much. Cora and Simmons knew in which direction he would ride. They knew that whatever it cost him, however bitter the bargain, he would come for Catana. 'I know,' Royal said. 'But there was nothing else I could do. They brought the girl with the light hair to the

147

ranch?'

'*Sí. Señora* Royal's new *del jurado* rode in with her some time ago. She is in the *casa* with *Señor* Mason and the *señora* now . . .'

'Is she all right?'

'*Sí, señor.* She is but bait for their trap.' The old man begged, 'Please to ride back to wherever you came from. Here there are many guns against you.'

'How many?' Royal asked.

The Mexican was vague. '*Cuarenta. Cincuenta.* Every bunk in the new bunkhouse is filled.'

Royal mulled over the information. Forty, fifty men. He would need a small army to take Catana out of the ranch house by force. But possibly, just possibly, one man could do it.

He eyed Manuel's sombrero, then the heavy blanket which the old man was wearing against the cool air of the evening. It wouldn't be much of a disguise. It might get him past the bunkhouse. If he could get into the house proper unobserved, he could equal the odds. Considering everything she stood to gain if the vote went in her favor on Tuesday, Cora couldn't risk the chance that a deceived husband would pull the trigger of the gun he was holding to her head. Not for the sake of one blond Mexican. If he could just get into the house unseen.

The major-domo protested vigorously but made the exchange.

Two of Cora's riders were sitting on the step of the bunkhouse. It was too dark to see their faces but the glowing tips of their cigarillos were plainly visible. Stooping as much as he could to disguise his height, Royal shuffled past them and across the courtyard to the open gallery and the lighted windows of what had been his home.

There'd been a number of changes since he'd left. All of the old comfortable and familiar furniture had been replaced by expensive and fragile-looking pieces. He supposed it was Cora's idea of how the drawing room of a lady of fashion should be furnished. Instead, it made the big room look more like the reception room of a high-class New Orleans bagnio.

Catana, looking very small and very frightened, was sitting on the edge of one of the green brocade covered chairs, her hands folded in her lap. Cora, wearing a long white silk peignoir, was reclining on a chaise longue. Hal Mason was leaning idly against the fireplace, his right hand resting on the well-worn butt of his gun. They all seemed to be waiting.

Royal shrugged off the blanket, drew his gun and started into the room. Then he stopped as the hard muzzle of a gun was thrust against the back of his head and Dijon asked:

'What detained you, Major? We knew you'd show up sooner or later.'

Under the prodding of the gun barrel, Royal stepped into the room and Catana rose from the chair and ran to him.

'I'm sorry,' the girl said. 'I did just what you told me to do. But after I heard the shots, I also believed the man when he said that you were dying and wanted to speak to me.'

'I know,' Royal said. He put his left arm around the girl but held on to his drawn gun in his right hand. He was fairly sure that Cora would not allow the man behind him to spatter his brains all over her new furniture. Possessions meant too much to her.

'All right, Cora,' he said. 'You knew I'd come. What's the deal?'

The black-haired woman was amused. 'I thought you'd ask that. But I'm afraid you're in for a disappointment, John. No one is going to offer you a deal. You don't have anything left to bargain with.'

'Then why stage the scene in Dry Prairie to get me out here?'

Cora admitted, 'Oh, you do have a certain nuisance value.' She laughed. 'Considering the size of the stakes I'm playing for, I can't afford to have even a husband galloping around the countryside playing Paul Revere and breaking prisoners out of jail.'

Royal said, 'It's a little late to do anything about the Johnsons.'

Cora shrugged. 'They're small fry. With you and that damn Yankee lawyer out of the way, no one will pay any heed to the Johnsons. Especially when you don't show up to vote the day after tomorrow and my men start a rumor that you decided you couldn't buck me after all and the last time you were seen, you were riding toward the border. You and your little blond Mexican whore.'

Dijon asked, 'Why not let me shoot him now, madame, and so end this little farce?'

'No,' Cora said. 'Not in here. Maybe not at all,' she mused. 'After all, I have nothing against the man personally.' It was a bitter memory. 'He did give me my start. He picked me out of a one-room adobe on the Brazos.'

Dijon sighed and gave a slight bow, 'As you say, madame.'

Cora went on. 'You see, John, while your coming back from the dead has made things embarrassing for me, you've never really been a problem. You're nothing but a former Johnny Reb who refused to take the oath. I could have let Dijon shoot you, instead of worrying you the way he has, and no one would have done anything to me or to him. It was Tyler who was the problem. He's a former Union soldier with excellent connections. So we had to give him enough rope to let him hang himself. And tonight, by breaking the Johnsons out of jail, he's made himself liable to a long term in federal prison. Who knows? Colonel Simmons may even have him shot.'

'No wonder it was so easy,' Royal said

151

bitterly.

Mason spoke for the first time. 'Like shooting fish in a pool. We've known what you were planning since last night. And if you ask me, those Union soldiers are good actors.'

Catana moved closer to Royal. 'What is she going to do with us?'

'I don't know,' Royal said.

Cora smiled. 'I'm not going to do a thing until after Tuesday. Then whatever I do will be legal. Maybe I'll let you both go.' She studied Catana's slim figure. 'Then again I may keep you here to entertain my riders.'

'No. Please, *señora*,' Catana begged.

Cora shrugged. 'Why be so fussy? What's one man more or less to a whore?'

'That,' Royal said, 'will be enough. Don't judge all women by yourself, Cora.'

'Or you'll do what?' the woman asked, and nodded to Dijon. Sensing what was about to happen Royal tried to turn and the barrel of Dijon's gun sliced down in a vicious blow that sent him to his knees clinging to Catana's legs for support. Then Dijon hit him again and all feeling left him and he sprawled face down on the floor.

CHAPTER SIXTEEN

When consciousness returned, Royal got to his feet with Catana's help and leaned against the wall until his head cleared. His vision was slightly blurred. He'd dropped his gun and Cora had scooped it up and was sitting on the edge of the chaise, regarding him thoughtfully.

'Or you'll do what?' she repeated.

Royal wiped at the blood on his face with his neckcloth. The lust for power and money did strange things to people. There was no limit to Cora's ambition. Nor was there anything he could do or say that would dissuade her from whatever she planned for him and Catana. She hated him because he was a link with the one-room adobe on the Brazos. While she wouldn't admit it even to herself, she was jealous of Catana. It hurt her pride to learn that he preferred another woman to her.

'I asked you a question,' Cora said, then turned her attention to the doorway as a horseman clattered across the courtyard unchallenged. A moment later, the commander of the Union garrison in Dry Prairie strode into the room.

Simmons looked at Royal and Catana, then crossed the room to the liquor cabinet and poured a large glass of whiskey.

153

'What are you in such a lather about?' Cora asked him. Simmons drank his whiskey, then he said, 'You know, Cora, there are times when I wish I'd never met you.'

'Make sense,' the black-haired woman said.

'All right,' Simmons said, 'I will.' He set his glass on the cabinet and took a paper from his pocket and unfolded it. From where Royal was standing, it looked like a duplicate of the ballot Jim Tyler had shown him the night before. Simmons traced his name with his finger. ' "For Governor—Colonel William Simmons." Tell me, Cora. Is it not customary to inform a candidate that he is running for office?'

The woman shrugged. 'I intended to tell you.'

'But not until after Tuesday.'

'Frankly, no.'

Simmons poured more whiskey into his glass. 'Because you knew I wouldn't stand for it.'

'Something like that,' Cora said. 'But where did you get hold of a ballot? I told that stupid printer not to let anyone see them until I called for them Tuesday morning.'

Simmons drank his second drink. 'So he told me when I got him out of bed. And he also confirmed something I'd learned elsewhere, that he'd given out one other ballot.'

'To whom?'

154

'To Mr. Kirby.'

Cora shrugged.

'And to whom do you think Mr. Kirby gave his ballot?'

'I haven't any idea.'

'He gave it to Jim Tyler.'

Cora looked puzzled. 'All right. Maybe I should have consulted you, Bill. But I don't see why you should be so upset about Mr. Kirby giving the ballot to Tyler.'

'I'll tell you why,' Simmons said. 'Do you have the faintest idea what will happen if and when the Judge Advocate General's Department sees this ballot?'

Cora's face was blank.

'They'll send a senior officer down here to go over my records. And when he does and finds out some of the things I've done he'll recommend a summary court-martial!'

Cora laid Royal's gun on the floor beside the chaise and leaned back with her hands clasped behind her neck. 'Aren't you exaggerating a little, Bill?'

Simmons took off his campaign hat. 'No. You see, the presumption is that for the last three years I've been administering this district by the book and not according to the whims of one Cora Royal. Can't you understand? This won't be a local matter any more. I'll be dealing with the Army. The United States Army. And when it becomes known that I'm running for civil governor of a newly formed state carved out of the military district of which I am in charge, I'm going to be in big trouble.'

'All right.' Cora became sullen. 'I'm sorry. But I had to put someone on the ballot I knew I could trust. And I felt that if I talked it over with you, you would never agree to run.'

'How right you are,' Simmons said.

'Now calm down and stop worrying,' Cora ordered. 'And, for heaven's sake, leave that whiskey bottle alone. We can handle the Army. You'll seen the whole thing will be over before the Judge Advocate General's office even hears about it.'

'It will?'

'Of course,' Cora assured him. 'This is Sunday night. The voting is scheduled for Tuesday. And as soon as the polls close, all you have to do is resign your commission and the military can't touch you.'

Simmons was grimly amused. 'You make it all sound so plausible. But I'm afraid if you want my help, you'd better hurry Tuesday along.'

'Why?'

'Because if you don't, I won't be here to help you. I'll be sitting in my own guardhouse.'

'What are you talking about?'

Simmons smiled wryly. 'After my men arrested Tyler, as we had planned, I questioned him and he didn't seem at all worried. In fact, he laughed at me.' Simmons crumpled the ballot into a ball and dropped it on the floor. 'You see, he'd already sent the ballot Mr. Kirby had given him to General Sheridan.'

Cora sat erect on the edge of the chaise. 'Then don't just stand there swilling whiskey. Order a detail to ride after his messenger and stop him.'

'I would, if I thought it would do any good,' the colonel said. 'But it's a little late. Thanks to Major Royal's insistence, Tyler's man left Dry Prairie last night. Right after they planned the jail break.'

Cora rose to her feet and walked over to where Royal was standing and slapped him across the face with the palm and again with the back of her hand. 'I should have let Dijon kill you.'

'So it would seem,' Royal said. 'But then, he has been trying to do that for months.'

The woman turned to Simmons. 'I think you're making too much of this, Bill. Even if Tyler's man did leave last night, he can't possibly reach New Orleans in time for anyone from the Judge Advocate's office to get here before the vote is in.'

Simmons rubbed the side of his nose with his empty glass. 'I wonder. When things are really going right a man can't lose for winning. But once things start to go sour—'

'Just what is that remark supposed to mean?' Cora interrupted. 'What else has gone wrong?'

'Tyler's man won't have to ride as far as New Orleans. The General is making a tour of inspection and right now he is in Nacogdoches.'

'He's coming here?'

'I doubt that he was planning on it. But he will when he sees that ballot. At least he'll send his adjutant.'

Cora paced the room, the frothy hem of her white negligee swishing around her bare ankles. 'Of all the rotten luck. I would make one stupid mistake. But I think I know the cure. Instead of waiting until Tuesday, we'll hold the balloting tomorrow. At best, the whole thing is only semi-legal. All I want is to get the vote on record. Then, if we have to, we'll throw the whole business into the courts. First, the state courts then the United States Supreme Court.'

Royal asked, 'Aren't you forgetting one thing, Cora? What if the rest of the state of Texas doesn't agree to the division?'

His former wife stopped pacing and faced him. 'I'm not worried about the rest of Texas. If the vote goes my way, the rest of Texas can go whistle. We'll be a separate state, at least technically. And according to the Eleventh Amend-ment, in the grant of jurisdiction to the Supreme Court, and I quote, "The judicial powers of the United States shall not be construed to extend to any suit in law or

158

equity, commenced or prosecuted against anyone of the United States by citizens of another state." Let the Supreme Court kick that around. Along with the proposition as to whether or not we had the right to exercise the franchise clearly stated in the original annexation treaty. It's certain to take months, possibly years, before the court can hand down a decision in either case. And by that time—'

Royal finished the sentence for her. 'By that time you will have stolen or gobbled up everything in this section of Texas but the prickly pear and the cactus.'

'That's right.' Cora was defiant about it. 'And if we are adjudged legally constituted as a state, I'll go right on stealing. One way or another, Texas will remember me.'

Royal wished he knew more about state and national law than he did. On the surface, Cora's presumptions were legally shaky. Still, in other sections of the state there were malcontents and hotheads who would back one section's right to secede. The legal and moral right of one section of the state to separate from the rest of Texas would be discussed and fought over in stores and saloons and in main streets from Brownsville to El Paso. It could drag on for years and the scars it left would be permanent.

He eyed the gun Cora had laid on the floor beside the couch. Even if he could get his hands on it he wouldn't stand much of a chance against Mason and Simmons and Dijon. But it might be the only chance he'd have. He took a step away from the wall and said, 'You can't do this, Cora.'

'I wouldn't bet on that if I were you,' she said. She nodded at Mason and Dijon. 'You two ride on into town and spread the word that I'm moving the vote up one day. But before you leave, put Major Royal and his Mexican tart in the storeroom.'

'Yes, ma'am,' Mason said.

As the other man moved away from the fireplace, Royal hurled himself across the few feet that separated him from the chaise and snatched the gun off the floor and rolled. But Mason was quicker and before he could trigger the gun the foreman took two quick steps forward and kicked it out of his hand.

'Nothing personal, understand,' Mason said. 'But I have quite a stake in this thing, myself.'

Dijon shrugged off Catana's attempt to stop him and kicked the man on the floor a vicious blow, first in the groin, then in the head. 'This is personal,' the one-time legionnaire said. 'I had a good thing going for me until you walked away from that firing squad.'

Catana knelt on the floor beside Royal and tried to shield him with her body.

'How touching,' Cora said. 'You can take them to the storeroom now. But if I may give you a word of advice, *señora*—'

The   kneeling   girl   looked   up

contemptuously.

Cora was amused. 'I know you may be tempted to spend the night in my former husband's arms. But you'd better use the time for praying.'

Catana tilted her small chin defiantly. 'Praying for what?'

Cora's face took on a look of pure malice. 'Praying that the vote goes right for us. Because if it doesn't, I'm afraid when we get back to the ranch tomorrow night, Colonel Simmons and I are not going to be in a very good mood.'

CHAPTER SEVENTEEN

The new storeroom that Cora had built was twice as large as the old one and smelled like a general store, of new blankets and tarred canvas, saddles and harness, chili peppers and onions, sacked and barreled provisions. There were also several freshly dressed sides of beef hanging from meat hooks on the wall.

Mason left them a lighted lantern but after several tours of the room, deciding it was impossible to dig through the thick adobe walls without a tool and equally as impossible to pry open the iron bars in the ventilation slots, Royal set the lantern on a barrel and spent what was left of the night sitting on a blanket with his back against the wall with Catana huddled close beside him for warmth.

The girl felt good in his arms. There was so much that he wanted to tell her, but it never seemed to be the time or the place for it.

Shortly before dawn, he heard the night wranglers bring in the remuda and he stood up and looked through one of the barred slots.

'What can you see?' Catana asked.

'Not much.'

There were lights in the bunkhouse now and as the morning grew older, men drifted out of the door and used the washbasins, cast speculative looks at the sky, then clustered in little groups smoking their first cigarillos of the day as they waited for the breakfast triangle to sound.

The day would be hot but the morning was still cool and spiced with the smell of frying steaks and side meat, tortillas and frijoles, johnny cake and freshly brewed coffee. The men were too far away for Royal to hear what they were saying but from time to time, one or more of the men glanced at the storeroom and made a remark and the others would laugh as at some private joke.

Her voice small, Catana said, 'She didn't mean what she said, did she? She wouldn't give me to her riders.'

'No. Of course not,' Royal lied.

'What will she do with us?'

'I don't know,' he said without turning.

He looked from the men to the main house as a pretty Mexican girl came out carrying two buckets of water and splashed the water on the floor of the gallery, then swept it. Manuel was supervising her work and as Royal watched, he thought: The old man is our only hope but it doesn't seem as though there is much he can do.

Manuel and the girl disappeared and a few minutes later Cora came out of the house wearing the same white negligee she'd had on the night before. She looked up at the sky and stretched, causing the front folds of the garment to open briefly. It was the only covering she had on.

Apparently, with success so near, Cora had given up all pretense of keeping her affair with Colonel Simmons a secret. He followed Cora out onto the gallery in his shirtsleeves, his suspenders dangling, more interested in working the cotton out of his mouth than he was in Cora or the weather.

As Royal watched, Manuel and the Mexican girl served breakfast to the two. Cora was using the heavy sterling silver coffeepot and the trays and covered dishes that his father had brought back as his part of the spoils from the looting of Monterey.

Royal gave Cora the credit due her. Whether she was stealing a few thousand of her neighbor's longhorns or a fifth of Texas, or entertaining her lover at breakfast, she did things on a grand scale. One remark she'd made last night had been true. Texas would remember her.

'What are they doing now?' Catana asked.

'Eating breakfast.'

'The *señora* and her lover?'

'That's right,' Royal said.

There was an edge to Catana's voice. 'Are you very sure you are not still in love with her?'

He shook his head impatiently. 'Don't be ridiculous.'

'Then why—' Catana began and thought better of what she'd been about to say.

Royal tried to read Simmons' face. The man was killing himself with liquor. His normally florid color was even redder than it had been the night before. His cheeks were bloated. He looked as if he'd spent the night paying more attention to the bottle than he had to Cora. His breakfast consisted entirely of coffee, both cups liberally laced with the contents of the bottle he'd carried out onto the gallery with him.

Simmons seemed to be angry about something, pounding one fist on the table to emphasize his points. Then when Manuel brought his horse, he went into the house and came out again wearing his hat and gauntlets, his well-tailored tunic buttoned into what approached military smartness. He mounted his horse and rode through the gate and down the road to Dry Prairie.

Cora sat at the table for a few minutes after he'd gone. Then, she, too, retired into the house, presumably to dress.

By seven o'clock the riders had finished their morning meal and had saddled their mounts and were congregating in the courtyard. Royal studied the faces he could see. Cora had chosen her private army well. Most of them looked like men who had nothing left to lose, men willing to do anything for one hundred dollars a month and their keep. It was small wonder that Nels Nielsen's young wife and the other small ranchers' wives were afraid of them.

A few minutes after seven, Cora reappeared on the gallery. It was to be her big day and she was dressed for it. She wore a wasp-waisted dress with a full skirt and a huge picture hat covered with flowers and carried a small ruffled parasol in one hand and her smart reticule in the other. In short, she looked like a lady.

As he watched, a team of matched bays drawing a black surrey with Chinese red wheels and a white fringe along its top appeared and stopped in front of the gallery. Hal Mason helped Cora into the surrey.

Cora looked at the driver of the surrey and asked, 'Where is Manuel?'

The Mexican in the driver's seat bobbed his head. 'Please to excuse him, *señora*. Manuel is *muy enfermo* and he transferred the honor of driving the *señora* to me.'

'Oh, no,' Cora said. 'I'm not leaving him here while I'm gone.' She dispatched Mason to locate Manuel. Then, with the aged major-domo on his accustomed seat in the surrey, Royal lost what little hope he'd had as Cora singled out one of her mounted men.

'You. What's your name?'

The burly rider rode up to the surrey. 'Goss. Charlie Goss, Mrs. Royal.'

'Oh, yes,' Cora said. 'I remember now.' She gave him his instructions. 'I want you to stay at the ranch and keep a sharp eye on the prisoners.'

The rider was disappointed. 'Whatever you say, Mrs. Royal. Do you want me to ask the cook to feed them?'

'That might be a good idea,' she answered him. 'But you go with the cook when he takes them their meal.' She wet her lips with the tip of her tongue. 'And if something should happen to the major and you have a little fun with the girl while we're gone, who's to know about it? All I'm interested in is that they are both here when I get back from Dry Prairie.'

'Yes, ma'am, Mrs. Royal.' Goss grinned. 'I'll see to that. They'll be here.'

Led and followed by the cavalcade of riders, the surrey passed through the gate. Royal watched it out of sight, then realized he was gripping the bars so hard his knuckles had

166

turned white. It didn't seem possible that he could have been so wrong about one woman.

He took his hands from the bars and turned to find Catana staring at him. 'You heard?' he asked her.

The girl averted her eyes. 'I heard.'

Royal searched through the storeroom again for some kind of a weapon, any kind of a weapon. This time, with more light to search by, he found what he was looking for. When the cook had come into the storeroom the night before to cut two steaks for Cora and Simmons to eat for supper, he'd left his thin-bladed knife stuck in the carcass of one of the beefs.

Royal tried the point, then the edge of the blade on his thumb. The knife would do nicely. The point and the edge were scalpel sharp. He put the knife inside his shirt and returned to where Catana was waiting.

'Do you trust me, Catana?'

The girl was hurt. 'I think you should know that by now.'

'Good,' Royal said. 'Here's what I want you to do.'

It was almost half an hour later when they heard footsteps outside the door. A moment later a key turned in the lock and the cook came in, followed by Goss. The rider wasn't taking any chances of being surprised. He had his gun in his hand with the hammer cocked.

Nodding curtly to Royal, Goss said, 'Mrs.

Royal thought you might like some grub.' He motioned for the cook to set the tray of food he was carrying on a pile of stacked sacks of flour, then glanced suspiciously around the room. 'All right. Don't be cute with me, Royal. Where's the little Mex girl?'

Royal spoke without expression, 'Lying on a pile of blankets back of those barrels, sleeping.' He added, 'She didn't get to sleep until almost dawn.'

'I'll bet. I'll just bet,' Goss said. 'You can go now,' he told the cook. 'And close the door behind you.' When the man had left, he made his position clear. 'Now, look. I don't want any trouble with you, Major. But you can have some if you want it. So, as I see it, you can do one of two things. You can eat your breakfast while I have a little fun with the girl. Or you can try to stop me and take a couple of slugs in the gut. It's up to you. All that Mrs. Royal said when she left was that she wanted you here when she came back from Dry Prairie.' Goss came closer. 'And like it says on the wanted flyers they got out on me, it don't make no mind whether you're dead or alive.'

'I see,' Royal said. He picked a piece of side meat from the tray and ate it. 'Well, seeing as I'm not packing one, I'd be a fool to argue with a gun.'

'Now you're talking sense,' Goss said.

The rider moved a step away from Royal and looked behind the barrels. He sucked in

168

his breath. He had good reason. Her new dress and pantaloons and *camisilla* wadded into a ball to form a pillow, Catana lay nude with her eyes closed, her small but beautiful breasts pointed up at the low ceiling as they rose and fell with her rhythmic breathing.

'Jesus,' Goss cursed thickly. 'I never knew they made them that pretty. And to think I was feeling sorry for myself because I had to stay behind.'

He felt the blade of the knife in Royal's hand prick his side and he stopped talking.

'Now, I'll give you your choice,' Royal said. 'You can lower the hammer, then drop the gun you're holding or you can take seven inches of steel. Remembering of course that I'm a surgeon and I'll know what to jab for.'

Goss looked, agonized, from the nude girl to Royal and made his decision. 'No. Please, Major. I was just having a little fun. I—I wasn't going to hurt either you or the girl.'

'The gun,' Royal said coldly. 'The gun.'

Perspiration beaded his cheeks as the big man lowered the hammer of his gun and dropped it. Catana opened her eyes and scrambled across the blanket and retrieved it.

'Did I do all right?' she asked.

'You did fine,' Royal assured her. 'Now as soon as you can dress, we're getting out of here.'

Goss protested, 'But you can't do that, Major. If you and the girl aren't here when

169

Mrs. Royal gets back she'll have Mason or Dijon kill me.'

'I couldn't care less,' Royal said. He dug the point of the knife a little deeper into the other man's side. 'Now suppose we step over to the door while I tie you up. It's not polite to watch a lady while she's dressing.'

Working rapidly, with some rawhide thongs he found hanging from a rafter, Royal bound Goss's wrists and ankles, then hogtied him to make sure he wouldn't cause them any more trouble.

While he was tying the final knot, Catana came out from behind the barrels, dressed now.

Royal took Goss's gun from her and spun the cylinder. All the chambers were filled.

He opened the door of the storeroom, then stepped out, with Catana following him. After he closed and locked the door, he led the way into the courtyard and looked around swiftly. The only one visible was Conchita, Cora's personal maid, who was standing on the gallery trying hard to pretend she hadn't seen them.

Gripping Catana's elbow, Royal crossed the courtyard to the gallery. 'Are there any horses up?' he asked the girl.

Conchita stopped pretending and curtseyed. '*Sí, señor. Señor* Goss's horse and the team the *señora* uses to draw the buckboard.'

'That will do fine,' Royal said.

170

With Catana walking beside him, he got the team from the corral, harnessed them to the buckboard, then led the team back to where Goss's saddled horse was standing.

No one shot out of a window or even called to him. Royal untied the horse, then helped Catana into the wagon.

'Now I want you to drive to Jim Tyler's ranch and wait for me,' he said. On impulse, he handed her most of the money Kirby had given him. 'But keep the team harnessed. And if I don't show up by an hour after nightfall, I want you to light out again and drive as fast as you can, night and day if need be, to Nacogdoches and put yourself under the protection of the Union garrison there.'

The girl studied his face. 'And you—?'

Royal stuffed Goss's gun into his empty holster. 'I'm riding into Dry Prairie.'

She protested, 'But they may hang you for helping those men escape.'

'Even so,' Royal said grimly. 'This thing must be settled one way or another today.'

Catana unwrapped the reins from the butt of the whip. 'Then I am going with you.'

'No,' Royal said. 'You'll do just what I told you to do.'

The girl looked at him defiantly for a moment, then lowered her eyes and began to cry. 'Whatever you say. You are the man.'

Royal wished he knew why she was crying. He wished he knew how to comfort her.

Thinking of her as she lay on the blanket pretending to be asleep was still agony. During the long night just past, while she lay in his arms, soft and warm, despite his fierce desire to possess her, because she was so dear to him, he hadn't even kissed her.

He wondered if he would ever know why she'd been so generous in his cell in San Rosario. But even that didn't alter the fact that she was a lady. And he'd been treating her like the little lady that she was.

CHAPTER EIGHTEEN

Dijon and Mason had done a good job in spreading the word that the voting had been moved up a day. The closer Royal came to town the more horses and rigs there were on the road.

More important, not only the town element and the would-be office seekers in the proposed new state were on the move. Small and large ranch owners for miles around had hitched up their buggies and buckboards and their spring wagons and were bringing their women and children with them. They might or might not have the nerve to vote against Cora and her riders, the colonel and his troopers, but they were concerned about the proposed separation.

Royal rode across the loose board planking above Gilmore Creek and down the single main street, making no attempt to conceal his identity. Considering the number of interested parties there were in town, he doubted that Cora would have him killed there. Further, with one of the ballots probably in the hands of General Sheridan by now, Simmons would avoid arresting him for assisting the Johnsons escape. Neither the colonel nor Cora wanted open war. They knew, they had to know, that they were sitting on a keg of dynamite and the smallest spark would ignite it.

Royal rode through the boisterous business section to the calm of the blacksmith shop and the courthouse, then turned his horse and rode through the clump of cottonwoods up to the row of barred windows on the near side of the guardhouse and called softly:

'You in there. Which cell are you in, Jim?'

Tyler came to one of the windows and looked through the bars. 'I'm glad to see you, John. But you're a damn fool. You shouldn't be here. Your wife's riders will shoot you on sight.'

'My ex-wife's riders,' Royal corrected him. 'And if I'm shot at, you can bet your bottom dollar that I'll shoot right back and they know it. I just stopped by to tell you to sit tight. If the vote goes the way we want it to, I'll have you out of here by sundown.'

Tyler was practical. 'And if it doesn't?'

'We'll think of something,' Royal said.

Tyler gripped the bars of his cell. 'I hope so. It would be rather ironic if, after living through five years of fighting you rebs from Manassas to Cape Fear, I swung for helping to pry three of you out of a Union guardhouse. But tell me this, Royal. Why did they move the vote up to today?'

Royal explained, 'Time is pinching out on them. Simmons has to get the vote in and resign his commission before he faces a court. And from the way he talked and acted last night, he expects his replacement to ride in with new troops as soon as General Sheridan sees that ballot.'

Tyler thought a moment. 'But that won't affect the vote today.'

'No,' Royal agreed. 'But the country people for miles around are swarming into town. All the roads leading into Dry Prairie are alive with rigs and riders. And while I have a feeling that they're hesitant about voting one way or another, it may be I can set an example.'

'How? By getting yourself killed?'

'No,' Royal said. 'I'm going to try to keep that from happening.' He swung his horse's head away from the window. 'Well, I'll see you later, I hope.'

'I hope,' Tyler echoed him.

Royal rode past the front of the courthouse and back into town unchallenged.

The pianos were still tinkling. The saloons

174

were crowded and noisy. The sidewalks were just as crowded. The same whores in their same flimsy wrappers sat in their windows displaying their dubious charms and calling to the men below them.

But there was a subtle difference in the feel of the place. Amid the drunks and the gamblers, the pimps and office seekers and Cora's gunmen, tight little clusters of serious men in their work clothes, men with weathered faces and calluses on their hands, their gunbelts strapped around their lean hips, formed small islands of indecision, apprehension and, above all, respectability.

Only one factor was conspicuously absent. There was not one soldier in sight. For some reason, Simmons had confined his troops to their quarters.

Royal reined in his horse before the hotel and sat looking up at the banner stretched across the street. It read: POLLING PLACE—VOTE HERE.

He dismounted and hitched his borrowed horse to the rail. It became instantly obvious to him why the better element in the county was reluctant to vote. A man had to pass through a double line of cold-eyed gunmen, whom Cora had stationed on either side of the hotel door, in order to vote.

As Royal stepped up on the walk the man nearest him dropped his hand on the butt of his gun. *'Un momento,* Major. You aren't supposed to be here.'

'That's right,' Royal said. 'I'm supposed to be back in the storeroom on the ranch. But I got tired of playing prairie dog, so I exchanged places with Goss. And now I'm going in and vote. Have any of you gentlemen any objection?'

The rider who'd spoken to him hesitated, then shrugged and stepped aside.

Royal strode across the walk and into the hotel lobby and stopped behind the last man in the line of men waiting to cast their votes. There were eight of them. Judging from the way they were dressed and the degree of their sobriety, Royal figured six yes and two no votes. Considering the odds, the two votes wouldn't amount to much but the sight of the two no voters made Royal feel better. He was glad there were a few men left in Texas who were willing to vote their convictions.

Royal moved with the line of men up to the ballot box and the two curtained-off polling booths on either side of the election judge's desk, where Cora was sitting with Dijon and Mason. Cora was the first to see him. Color crept into her cheeks and there was a tight quality to her eyes. She demanded of him, 'How did you get here?'

'That,' Royal said, laughing, 'is a long story. But I think it's obvious why I'm here. After all, this is a free election. Or is it?'

'I'll take care of him, madame,' Dijon said.

176

'I will do that which you should have permitted me to do some days ago.'

He started to rise to his feet and the black-haired woman said tersely, 'Not in here, you fool. This thing can go either way. If you kill him in here that whole crowd of psalm-singing sodbusters might just swarm over us like a pack of wolves. I don't want any trouble, *any* trouble, understand, until the vote is in.'

'I figured that,' Royal said cheerfully.

Cora looked back at Royal and said icily, 'Well, if you're going to, vote.'

Royal touched the brim of his hat. 'Sorry. I've changed my mind, Cora. If you have no objection, I think I'll postpone voting until later in the day. As I understand it, according to law, the polls have to stay open until six o'clock. And right now, I think I'll take a little walk around and see if I can't drum up a few votes for our side. But I'll be back.'

Dijon again fingered the butt of his gun. 'We'll be here. And while I don't know how you got out of the storeroom, I can tell you this much. If you are as smart as you think you are, instead of coming here, you'd have kept right on riding.'

'We'll see,' Royal said. 'We'll see.'

CHAPTER NINETEEN

As the day grew hotter, Royal had the uneasy impression that time had been suspended, that he was moving through a superheated area of space in slow motion.

It had been a few minutes after ten o'clock when he'd ridden into Dry Prairie. Now, at four o'clock, the drunks were still staggering from saloon to saloon, the tarts, when not otherwise engaged, were still calling from their windows and the tight little clusters of men on the walks were still talking.

Royal moved on, doggedly, through the heat and the dust and the confusion. Nine-tenths of the men he'd talked to were bitterly opposed to the separation and to Cora's hand-picked slate of candidates to fill the new offices. But they were all afraid to vote no because of almost certain reprisals. They argued that the vote on the proposal was only quasi-legal, the courts probably wouldn't support it and they had their ranches and families to think of.

Royal almost wished he hadn't come home. Or now that he had, that he'd said the hell with the ranch and with Dry Prairie and had ridden on to New Orleans with Catana. Good doctors were always in demand in New Orleans. He could have established an excellent practice in a year or two. He could even have married Catana. If she'd have him. After all, thirty-five wasn't old. If he and Catana should have children he'd only be fifty-six when their first-born was twenty-one. It would be nice to have a son.

It was something to think about. It still wasn't too late. He could ride out to Jim Tyler's ranch and he and the girl could be on their way in an hour. But then what would happen to Tyler? What would happen to his fellow townsmen? He'd brought Cora into the district. He was a Royal. It was the old army game all over. If rank had its privileges, it also had its responsibilities.

He walked on to the next group of men, his nerves taut from the mounting tension. He no longer had any illusions. This could well be the end as far as he was concerned. His own people, by failing to act, might well bring about what five years of civil war and a Mexican firing squad had failed to accomplish. As long as he was alive, the legality of Cora's claim to the ranch would always be in question. Cora was too smart and too unscrupulous to allow him to ride out of town. He'd never been a particularly fast man with a gun and the odds were ten to one that sometime before nightfall he would have to face Mason or Dijon.

The men in this group were no different from the men in any of the other groups with whom he'd talked. Most of them were against the proposal to split off from the rest of Texas. They despised Cora. They agreed that Colonel Simmons was playing it smart by keeping his troopers out of town and away from the voting booths. This way there could be no possible charge that the voters of Dry Prairie had been intimidated or coerced.

However, as a grizzled rancher pointed out, 'They's a hull camp of 'em just out of town. And Simmons knows we know it. Then there's Mrs. Royal's boys. And if the vote don't go the way she wants it to go, tonight, tomorrow night, or the night after that, when we're split up and alone, there's going to be a lot more barns and houses burned and a lot more cattle run off. As I see it, by standing up to be counted, all we're doing is sticking our necks out. And that's why I think we're better off to just sweat it out until the courts settle this thing.'

At five o'clock, Royal gave up and entered the Mired Mule Saloon and ordered a glass of beer. Most of the men at the bar were pro-Cora but none of them paid any attention to him. They didn't know who he was.

The beer tasted good. Royal drained his glass and ordered another. He thought, at least he'd tried. And what had happened? Not even the three Johnsons had shown up as they'd promised.

Someone crowded in beside him and he glanced sideways and recognized Mr. Kirby.

'How about one on me?' the banker asked.

'Thanks,' Royal said, 'but I'm working on my second one now and after dilly-dallying around all day, it's time I do something practical.'

Kirby ordered a beer for himself. 'Such as?'

'Such as voting. And maybe telling one or more of Cora's crooked election judges what I think of them.'

Kirby sipped his beer. 'I don't think that would be very smart, Major.'

'No, probably not,' Royal admitted. 'But at least I'll be on record.'

The banker tried to justify his position. 'Sure. That's all right for you, John. The way things have turned out you have nothing left to lose. But the rest of us are in a tight squeeze. Take me. I have my bank to think of.'

Royal finished his beer and set the glass back on the bar. 'And just what makes you think you'll have a bank in the morning? What makes you think your bank is safer than old man Johnson's longhorns?'

He pushed himself away from the bar and walked out onto the street. The news concerning his inevitable showdown with Dijon had had all day to spread. The walk was crowded but not for him. Men stepped aside to give him room.

He'd almost reached the hotel when he heard the footsteps behind him and glanced over his shoulder. Worried but determined,

Kirby was dogging his footsteps.

Royal waited for him to catch up. 'What's the idea?'

'I'm not quite sure,' the banker laughed without mirth. 'Maybe you shamed me back there. Maybe I'm worried about my bank. Then again, maybe I hate to see a good man go up against a stacked deal without one friend to side with him.'

'Thanks. Thanks a lot, Mr. Kirby,' Royal said.

He eased the gun in his holster and walked on. The gauntlet of men intended to discourage a rush of 'no' votes had disbanded. Cora's men were relaxing on the edge of the walk or sitting in chairs they'd brought from the lobby. They were laughing and passing premature victory bottles from hand to hand.

No one bothered to get to his feet as Royal and Kirby turned into the lobby.

His former wife showed her usual thin smile. 'I wondered if you'd have the nerve to come back. Just how did you make out in your little walkaround to drum up votes for your side?'

'He got at least one,' Mr. Kirby said.

Taking a printed ballot from the table, the banker wrote a precise 'no' in the proper space, then folded the ballot carefully and slipped it into the slot in the ballot box.

'I'll remember that, Mr. Kirby,' Cora said.

Kirby stepped back to allow Royal to mark

his ballot. 'I'm certain you will, Mrs. Royal.'

As Royal reached for a ballot, the one-time prison *comandante* of San Rosario got to his feet, resting his right hand on his gun.

'Any time you're ready, Major Royal.' He cocked his gun. 'I've waited a long time for this. Too long.'

Cora caught at Dijon's arm to stop him and succeeded only in deflecting his aim. The two bullets he managed to trigger dug holes in the floor at Royal's feet but the bullets from Royal's gun thudded solidly into the Frenchman's chest.

The sound of the bullets was followed by a tense silence. Then, with an incredulous look on his face, Dijon looked at Cora. 'You've killed me, madame,' he said. Then, as if he were very tired, he slid down in his chair, put his arms on the table and laid his head on them.

With an effort Royal turned his attention to Mason. 'If I were you, I wouldn't try what you're thinking. I'm not really fast. Thanks to Mrs. Royal, I was lucky. But if you want to pick up where Captain Dijon left off, you won't leave me any choice.'

Mason chose his words with care. 'In that case,' he put his hands on the table, 'I'll pass. Anyway, for now.'

'That's sensible,' Kirby said.

Without bothering to look behind him, Royal returned his gun to its holster, picked up a pencil and scrawled a big 'NO' across one of the ballots and stuffed it through the slit in the box.

He turned to leave and found the hotel doorway blocked by Cora's riders, so recently celebrating in the bars. None of them seemed to know quite what to do.

Cora Royal made up their minds for them. 'Let the major and Mr. Kirby go through. Dijon only got what he had coming. I told all of you I didn't want any avoidable trouble until the poll closes. We have a half hour to go.'

The riders stepped aside to allow Royal and Kirby to pass. Royal crossed the walk and stood a moment with his hand resting against one of the uprights supporting the overhang. His knees felt weak. He felt let down and put upon. This wasn't his fight alone nor the fight of the few men who had voted against the proposal. Every man in the street, staring back at him, had just as much at stake.

Cora had followed him and Kirby out onto the walk. In an attempt to regain any ground she might have lost, the black-haired woman scoffed, 'There they are, men. Take a good look at your heroes. One ex-Confederate Army surgeon without patients and not much of a future. And one brave banker who is about to lose his bank. They both voted no. Now, how many of the rest of you want to go on record and have some of my boys drop in on you tonight?'

184

The shots had gathered the scattered clusters of men into one large group in front of the hotel. Muttering angrily, the men in back pushed forward while the men in front, facing the armed gunmen on the raised walk, attempted to push back.

Cora was amused. 'I thought so. Now if you men out there in the street know what's good for you and your families, you'll climb back in your rigs and—' She stopped talking as three whooping horsemen, followed by a rapidly approaching ranch wagon with one dry wheel, clattered down the street and stopped on the edge of the crowd.

The horses the three Johnsons were riding were lathered with sweat. So was the Nielsen team. Unless Royal was seeing things, there, sitting on the swaying spring seat of the wagon beside Nels and Mrs. Nielsen and wearing the same too large woolen shirt and the tight vaquero pants she'd worn during the flight from San Rosario, was Catana.

Old man Johnson and his two hulking sons got down from their horses and elbowed their way through the crowd to where Royal and Kirby were standing.

'Sorry to be late to the festivities, gents,' the old man said. He took deliberate aim and spat a mouthful of tobacco juice against one of the red wheels of Cora's fringed surrey. 'But we was all set for tomorrow and moving the vote up a day kinda caught us with our britches off our saddles.' He inclined his head toward the blond girl sitting on the Nielsen wagon. 'Fact is, if the little *señorita* hadn't spent most of the day driving from ranch to ranch a-trying to round up some of his friends to side with the major, we might have missed the fun.'

Cora nodded to one of her men. 'Ride down to the courthouse and tell Colonel Simmons that the three prisoners who escaped the other night are back in town.'

Johnson helped the rider untie his horse. 'You do that, sonny. And after you tell him we're here, tell him we're all carrying repeating rifles and two leg guns and when him and his boys come for us, they damn well better bring along a cannon.'

The rider said, 'You don't mean that. You wouldn't dast fight the army.'

Johnson wiped tobacco juice from his white mustache with the back of one hand. 'We fit 'em for five years.' He paused as if in thought. 'And come to think of it, I never did surrender.'

A wave of nervous laughter rippled through the crowd of ranchers standing in the street. Elijah Johnson hiked up his gunbelt and grinned proudly at Royal. 'Pa's an old snoozer, ain't he, Major?'

Royal studied Catana's face. He was grateful to her for what she had done, but puzzled as to why she'd changed into the old blue shirt and tight pants. 'An old snoozer,' he agreed. 'Thanks for coming, boys.'

'Hit's a pleasure,' the elder Johnson said. He looked up at the banner stretched across the street, then back at Royal. 'Now just where do we vote "no" on this fool proposition?'

Royal inclined his head toward the door of the hotel. 'Inside the lobby, Orin. You'll find ballots and a ballot box on the table.'

'Good,' Johnson said. He looked reprovingly at his sons. 'Well, don't stand there catching flies with your mouths. We come to vote. Let's go do 'er.'

The three big men waded through the dust, shoulder to shoulder, while the gunmen on the walk seemed uncertain just what to do. At the last moment, they moved aside and the Johnsons stepped up on the walk and strode into the lobby of the hotel.

For a few seconds Royal was hopeful that first a trickle and then a rush of ranchers would follow them. But neither the trickle or the rush materialized.

Cora showed her contempt for the crowd of men facing her. 'Sheep. That's what you are. A flock of curly little lambs who deserve to be fleeced.'

She turned to re-enter the hotel but turned back as young Mrs. Nielsen spoke from the spring seat of the wagon. The young woman had changed her mind since Royal had last talked to her.

'Well?' she asked her husband. 'You heard

187

what that hussy called you, Nels. Are you just going to sit here with us women or are you going to vote? It's up to you. But if you think I'm going to let a woman who has her breakfast in a peek-a-boo white nightgown, out of covered silver dishes, after spending the night with a pair of boots that don't belong to her lawful, wedded husband under her bed, have the say of how much food and milk my younguns can have, and kin they live in Texas, you've got another think coming.'

The young woman paused for breath. Then she went on, 'Now you go in there and make your mark or else find a new bed to sleep in tonight. Acause iffen you don't vote "no" you purely ain't sleeping in mine.'

In the silence that followed, Nels Nielsen got down from the wagon, eyed the wall of gunmen on the walk, then hitched the gun on his own thigh forward.

As he did, someone on the fringe of the crowd spoke up. It was Mrs. Purdy, the wife of the owner of the Bon Ton who said, shrilly, 'That goes for you, too, Tom Purdy. Before that black-haired cat got her claws into us, Dry Prairie was a nice, peaceful, law-abiding town. A town you could be proud to raise your children in. Might just be we can make it that way again. Now you march yourself in there and vote.'

Other women were calling to their husbands now. The men in front of the crowd had

188

stopped pushing back and were edging forward, hoping there wouldn't be any trouble but ready for it if it came.

No longer amused, Cora Royal screamed at her riders. 'Well, what the devil are you standing there for? Stop them. Shoot them if you have to.'

Royal was never certain which side fired first. He believed it came from the street and that Nels Nielsen did it. He knew the gunman standing beside him threw up his arms and pitched forward off the walk into the dust, the gun he'd drawn on Cora's orders falling from his fingers as he dropped.

An uneven fusillade followed the first one. Then the two groups of men were too close to each other to use their guns as anything but clubs. It was dirty, vicious infighting. Cora's men fought back the best they knew how, but they were fighting for one hundred dollars a month and their keep, while the finally aroused ranchers were fighting for their families and their homes and the right to live and die in Texas.

Caught in a cross-fire between the three Johnsons inside the hotel and the angry men on the street, the riders didn't last long. One by one, realizing they were on the short end of the stick now, they broke out of the crowd and raced for open doorways or for their horses. Some of them made it.

As the fighting slackened, Kirby broke his

derringer and thumbed fresh shells into the chamber. 'Well, that seems to tear the rag.'

Breathing heavily from his efforts, Royal mopped at the blood trickling from the reopened wound on his head. 'So it seems,' he panted. 'It also seems that the sheep came out quite well.'

CHAPTER TWENTY

The tinkling of pianos had ceased. The girls had left their windows. There was an occasional flurry of shots as the ranchers flushed a paid rider from under a bed or from behind a bar.

Pushed this way and that by the jubilant men jostling each other for places in the long queue of men waiting to vote, Cora Royal stood, white-faced with anger, watching the dissolution of her dream. Then she picked up her long skirt to keep from snagging it on the boards of the walk and made her way through the confusion and hurried toward the court-house and Bill Simmons' headquarters.

'What now?' Kirby asked Royal.

Royal wanted to talk to Catana. There were several things he wished to ask her and more he wished to tell her. But before he did, he had one last matter to settle.

'I'm not quite sure,' he said to Kirby. 'We'll

190

decide that when I come back. If I come back.'

With a last look at Catana, he followed Cora down the walk to the courthouse. She went in and Royal started in after her but stopped as a Union major and two grizzled sergeants rode up to the hitching rail in front of the guardhouse and dismounted. Judging from the dust on their uniforms and the condition of their mounts, the three men must have ridden far.

Royal hoped they were who he thought they were. He went into the courthouse and down the hall leading to Colonel William Simmons' office. Looking older and more dissipated than when Royal had last seen him, Simmons was trying to be patient with Cora.

'I don't care how it looks,' she said hotly. 'We can't afford to have a "no" vote go into the record. So here's what I want you to do. Order a detail of your men to ride up to the hotel and disperse the crowd and impound the ballot box.'

Simmons sounded tired. 'You know I can't do that, Cora. I told you right from the start that we weren't going to get away with this. And the last half hour has proved me right.' He looked up and saw Royal. 'Oh,' he said quietly. 'I've rather expected you all day, Major. I'll be at your service in just a minute.'

'Oh, for heaven's sake,' Cora was sarcastic. 'Here everything I've worked toward for years is being torn down by an unwashed mob and all you can think of is your fool honor.'

Simmons sighed. 'I'm sorry, my dear. That's about all I have left. And I'm afraid that is rather badly tarnished.' He realized the corporal of the guard had emerged from the guardroom and was standing at stiff attention. 'Yes, Corporal?'

The corporal reported, 'A Major Durban and two staff sergeants have just ridden in from Nacogdoches, sir. And the major requests an immediate conference with you. He said to inform you that he is attached to the Judge Advocate General's office and you would understand.'

'Only too well,' Simmons said. 'Give the major my compliments and tell him I will see him in a minute.'

'Yes, sir.'

Simmons answered Cora's unspoken question. 'That's right. That damned ballot. I tried to tell you last night that headquarters was going to take a dim view of one of their military officers running for civil governor of the district of which he is in charge.' He bowed stiffly to Royal. 'You'll pardon me for giving this other matter preference but it seems there is something I have to do. Now if both of you will excuse me . . .'

He tried to close the door of his office but Cora caught at his arm. 'I don't give a good goddamn how many majors have ridden down from Nacogdoches. Right now there is nothing

192

more important than dispersing that mob and impounding that ballot box.'

Gently, Simmons lifted her hand from his arm and kissed it. 'Don't think it hasn't been fun, Cora. It has. But there is always a bill for everything we do. And sometimes it comes high.'

Then, before Cora could stop him, he released her hand and closed the door of his office and locked it.

Cora pounded on the glass. 'You have to listen to me, Bill.'

Fairly certain of what Simmons intended to do, Royal rattled the doorknob, then called loudly, 'Corporal. Corporal of the guard.'

The corporal, accompanied by the major and the two sergeants who'd just arrived, hurried down the hall and reached the door just in time to hear the shot.

'Break down that door,' the major ordered.

The sergeants did as they were told. Cora took one look into the office and began to cry. Royal didn't bother to look. He knew what Simmons had done. No detail would ever arrest him. No court-martial would ever strip him of his buttons and his commission and order him drummed out of the army that at one time in his life he'd served so well. Insofar as was humanly possible, Colonel William Simmons, U.S.A., had paid his share of the bill in full.

Royal introduced himself to Major Durban

and asked for permission to talk to him about Jim Tyler and the Johnsons later in the evening. Then he escorted Cora up the street toward the hotel.

There was a lot to be done before Dry Prairie would return to normalcy but while he and Cora had been in the courthouse, the sporadic firing had stopped and by some happy inspiration, someone had thought of ringing the church bells. The bell in the Baptist steeple and those in Father Alejandro's mission were pealing joyfully.

Cora broke the silence between them. 'I suppose,' she said, 'it wouldn't do a bit of good to say I'm sorry.'

'No,' Royal said.

She tried again. 'But I'm your wife.'

He corrected her. 'Former wife. Remember? You divorced me.'

They were alone when they started from the courthouse—but not for long. A crowd of angry women, women whose husbands Cora had humiliated, whose cattle she'd stolen, whose houses and barns she'd burned or had burned, whose land she'd confiscated, fell in step with them, cat-calling and jeering.

'Shame us, would you? . . . Steal our cattle? . . . Burn our barns? . . . Try to run us off our land? . . . We ought to boil up a pot of tar, strip you down to your dirty little hide and tar and feather you, then ride you out of town on a rail.'

194

With her eyes straight ahead, attempting to ignore the cat-calls and the threats, Cora plodded on. When they reached the white-fringed surrey Royal helped her into the front seat, then untied the team and handed her the lines.

'They mean what they say,' he told her.

'Yes,' Cora answered, tight-lipped. 'I know.'

Royal continued, 'Besides the threat to your personal safety, there will undoubtedly be legal repercussions as soon as Major Durban has had time to sort out the facts. So, if I were you, Cora, I'd get out of town as fast as I could and drive as far as I could.'

Cora's voice was bleak. 'Drive where? Where can I go?'

'That's up to you. How about going back to the Brazos?'

'I'd rather die.'

'Nacogdoches or New Orleans, then?'

'Either one of them would be better.' Her lower lip quivered. 'But how will I get there? I spent all the money I had on my riders. And what about my beautiful clothes?'

Royal considered the matter. He was no longer legally responsible for Cora but he wanted her out of his life, for good. He didn't want any dangling loose ends. The farther she went from Dry Prairie the more secure he would feel. 'I'll tell you what,' he said. He gave Cora the rest of the money he'd borrowed from Kirby. 'Why don't you try for New

Orleans? This should last you for some months. And if you write me from wherever you are I'll send your clothes.' He added, 'For that matter, if you want it, I'll clear out all that fool furniture you bought for the ranch and have it freighted on to you.'

Cora put the bills and the gold coins in her reticule. 'In other words, I have no choice. As a committee of one, you are running me out of Dry Prairie.'

'Let's just say I think it will be best for all concerned if you leave.'

Cora tightened the reins and backed the team away from the rail. 'In that case, I'd better get started.' A touch of her old bravado returned. 'It may be I'll find some place to spend the night.'

'I'm certain you will,' Royal said.

He watched the surrey move down the street. One couldn't help but admire the black-haired beauty. She drove with her back erect, her chin tilted, looking neither to right nor left. As far as outward appearance was concerned, she might have won instead of lost her gamble. One thing was plain. Wherever she decided to stop she would do well. Whatever she did she would do in the grand manner. However unfavorable the memory might be, Texas would always remember her.

Royal was suddenly conscious of being very tired and hot and thirsty. It had been a long day. There was more to do before the day was ended. Major Durban would want the answer to a lot of questions before he would release Jim Tyler. Those of Cora's riders who'd gotten away would have to be rounded up. But all of that could wait. It still wasn't quite the time or place but right now he had something he had to do.

Royal looked for and found the Nielsen wagon. Nielsen had tied his team in the shade on the far side of the street. Neither Nels nor his wife was in the wagon. They were part of the boisterous local crowd moving about in the street and on the walks, the men laughing and slapping each other on the back while their wives exchanged notes on their children and assured each other how wonderful things were going to be from now on. Especially with longhorns selling in Abilene for fourteen dollars a head.

Catana, however, was still sitting on the spring seat, in the midst of but not one of the crowd. She was trying to smile but her small face was swollen. She looked as if she'd been crying.

Royal walked over to the wagon. 'I want to talk to you, Catana.'

The little Mexican girl looked down at him coldly. 'There is no one stopping you.'

'I mean in private,' Royal said.

She shrugged her shoulders. 'We have been in private a number of times without you having this desire.'

'All right,' Royal said. 'We'll talk here. First I want to thank you for rounding up the Nielsens and the Johnsons. Then I want you to tell me why you are wearing those godawful pants and shirt instead of the pretty things I bought you.'

Catana's face turned sullen. 'That is, how you say, none of your business. But if you must know they are more convenient in which to travel.'

'Travel?' Royal puzzled.

Catana bobbed her head. '*Sí*. As soon as the Nielsens drive home and I can pick up the buckboard I left at their ranch, I am going back to Mexico.'

'And do what?'

The blond head shook and the shoulders were raised. 'How do I know? But I do know it would be better to be a cantina girl than to stay where one is not wanted.'

'Not wanted?' Royal exclaimed heatedly. 'What are you talking about?'

Catana tried not to cry and failed. 'If you do not know, I will tell you. The first night I saw you in San Rosario and you protected me, I went home and I dreamed all night. You were the sort of man that ever since I was a little girl I had prayed I would meet. You were so big. So gentle. So strong. Then when *Señor* Tyler asked me to carry the message to you in your cell I did so gladly.' She paused and her cheeks became pink. 'And if I was immodest with you

198

in your cell it was for two reasons. I was afraid if the guard became suspicious they might shoot you in the morning and because you had protected me I wanted to repay you.'

Once started talking she couldn't stop any more than she could stop crying. 'And the other reason was because just once in my life, I wanted to be loved by a man, a real man. Then when *Capitan* Dijon double-crossed *Señor* Tyler and Don Jesus and I had to flee with you, what did you do?'

'What did I do?' Royal was bewildered.

Catana sobbed harder. 'Nothing. That's what you did. Not once during all the weeks we were running away did you look at me as if I were a woman. Not once did you come to ne. But even then I said to myself, once we are safe it will be different. Then my lover will come to me and kiss me and hold me in his arms like he did in his cell. And I will tell him of my great love. But when we reached here, what happened?'

Royal was beginning to enjoy himself. 'Tell me.'

She continued to sob. 'First you walked into my room in the hotel while I was *desnudo*. And with me aching for you, you laid a dress and some things on my bed, then backed out and closed the door like an embarrassed boy.'

'I was.' Royal grinned. 'Embarrassed, I mean. Among other things.'

Catana went on, 'Then down in the dining

199

room, instead of letting me help you, you sent me to bed alone, like a child. And even last night at the ranch, not knowing if we would live or die by morning—'

'Now you look here, young lady,' Royal interrupted her. 'If I haven't spoken before, I had good reason. At least it seemed good to me. But—' He reached up and tried to lift her off the seat and she shook his hands away.

'No. Please not to touch me,' she said hotly. 'I do not ever want you to touch me again.' She took the money he had given her from the shirt and scattered it in the dust. 'Nor do I want the money you gave me.'

Ignoring the hands slapping at his, Royal lifted her bodily off the seat. 'You listen to me, fireball,' he said just as hotly. 'I'm sorry if I hurt your feelings. I know how you must have felt and I apologize for trying to be a gentleman. But now I'm going to prove to you just how I do feel about you.'

Catana kicked at his shins. 'How? By running *me* out of town?'

Still angry with her, Royal said, 'I'll show you how.' He put one booted foot on the nearest wagon wheel, then turned her over his knee. 'I'm going to take down your pants and spank you until you holler San Rosario. Then you and I are going over to the mission and ask Father Alejandro to marry us.'

He started to pull down the pants and the squirming girl blushed scarlet. 'No, please,

200

querido mío. Not here in the street. There is nothing under the pants and it would shame me with everybody watching.'

Royal looked up and was embarrassed too. They were no longer alone. Around them stood a circle of amused onlookers.

'Go ahead,' Johnson grinned. 'Smack her a few licks. It does a woman good from time to time.'

Catana continued to plead. 'No, please. I would be too ashamed.' Her voice became very low, 'Besides, it might hurt the *niño.*'

Royal lifted the girl off his knee and set her on her feet. 'Did you say *niño?* Did you say baby?'

Catana stuffed the tail of the shirt into her pants. 'But of course,' she said simply. 'What else would you expect of the hour we spent in your cell?'

As their lips met they had no need for words. As if from a great distance, the church bells were ringing and their friends' laughter was as gentle as spring rain falling on the prairie.

It was only fitting. After having been away for so many years, Major John Royal had come home.